THE SEVEN LAMPS

Jill Hartley has to take important papers to 18 Hayford Avenue, Berrydale, the home of her firm's client, Professor Locksley. But when she arrives at the neglected house she finds the front door open — the inside of the house, dark, damp and decaying. And huddled at the foot of the stairs lies a dead man, in a pool of blood, his head battered to a pulp. At Berrydale Police Station Superintendent Budd investigates this horrifying and mysterious case.

D1147818

Books by Gerald Verner
in the Linford Mystery Library:

THE LAST WARNING
DENE OF THE SECRET SERVICE
THE NURSERY RHYME MURDERS
TERROR TOWER
THE CLEVERNESS OF MR. BUDD

GERALD VERNER

THE
SEVEN
LAMPS

Complete and Unabridged

LINFORD
Leicester

First published in Great Britain

First Linford Edition
published 2011

British Library CIP Data

Verner, Gerald.
    The seven lamps.- -
    (Linford mystery library)
    1. Budd, Robert (Fictitious character)- -
    Fiction. 2. Police- -England- -Fiction.
    3. Murder- -Investigation- -England- -Fiction.
    4. Detective and mystery stories.
    5. Large type books.
    I. Title II. Series
    823.9'12–dc22

    ISBN 978–1–4448–0775–2

F. A. Thorpe (Publishing)
Anstey, Leicestershire

Set by Words & Graphics Ltd.
Anstey, Leicestershire
Printed and bound in Great Britain by
T. J. International Ltd., Padstow, Cornwall

This book is printed on acid-free paper

TO
MY WIFE
WITH LOVE

PART ONE

THE LAMPS OF THE GODS

1

'It is really very — er — kind of you, Miss Hartley,' said Mr. Tape in his dry, precise way, looking at the girl on the other side of the untidy desk through his spectacles. 'Very — er — kind of you indeed. It is most important that these documents should reach Professor Locksley tonight, and, since they are of considerable value, I do not care to entrust them to any ordinary messenger. If my chief clerk had not unfortunately — er — contracted influenza I should not have — er — had to make this request . . . '

Jill Hartley smiled, and it was a very attractive smile, as quite a number of the male sex had told her with varying degrees of eloquence.

'I don't mind in the least, Mr. Tape,' she said. 'I'm not doing anything this evening, anyway.'

'It is extremely kind of you all the same,' said the solicitor. 'I do not like, as a rule, to encroach upon the leisure hours of my employees. But this is an exceptional case — a very exceptional case. It would be in order, I think, Miss Hartley, for you to take tomorrow morning off in compensation for the — er — extra hours which you will spend in my service this evening.'

'Thank you very much, but that really isn't necessary,' she said. 'I don't mind in the least . . . '

'I should feel less under an obligation to you,' said Mr. Tape with dignity. 'We will, therefore, take it as settled that you will — er — not appear at the office until after luncheon tomorrow. Are you — er — acquainted with Berrydale?'

Jill shook her head, and Mr. Tape drew a slip of paper towards him with a lean hand, and, bending forward, peered down at it.

'There is an electric train from Waterloo at six-forty-two,' he said. 'That will give you time to have a — er — meal before you go. It gets to Berrydale at seven-twenty-three. Hayford Avenue is some three minutes' walk from the

4

station. You — er — turn left when you come out of the station, and keep straight on until you reach a roundabout. Hayford Avenue leads off from the roundabout almost facing the road from the railway station. You — er — cannot possibly miss it. Professor Locksley's house is number eighteen. I have — er — drawn a rough map for your guidance . . . ' He picked up a second slip of paper, and, reaching over the desk, gave it to her.

'I don't suppose I shall have any difficulty in finding the house,' said Jill, glancing at the neatly-drawn plan. 'I can always ask . . . '

Mr. Tape's bald head nodded slowly.

'You will take the necessary money for your — er — expenses from petty cash,' he said, opening a drawer beside him and taking out a long envelope, heavily sealed. 'You will deliver this to Professor Locksley, personally,' he went on gravely, 'and you will — er — get a receipt. There is no need for me to warn you, Miss Hartley, to take the greatest possible care of it. The — er — documents are of the utmost importance . . . '

'You can trust me, Mr. Tape,' said Jill, taking the bulky envelope.

'If I was not completely certain of that,' said the lawyer, removing his spectacles and polishing them delicately with a silk handkerchief, 'I should not have asked you to go.' He put on his spectacles again and consulted a thin gold watch. 'It is now half-past five,' he said. 'If you go now you will have plenty of time to — er — eat your meal. Food should — er — never be rushed. It should be masticated — er — like the — er — mills of God — slowly but exceeding small.'

It was a pet joke of Mr. Tape's, and Jill had heard it dozens of times before, but she dutifully laughed all the same.

2

Jill Hartley had a combined meal that was a mixture of tea and dinner in a restaurant in the Strand and, if she did not entirely emulate the mills of God, she at least she took her time over it. She had been with the firm of Messrs. Tape, Redman and Tape for over three years, two of which had been spent in the capacity of private secretary to Mr. Horatio Tape, the only surviving member of the original firm. A remarkable ability for swift and accurate shorthand, and an unusual interest in law, had got her the position, and she thoroughly enjoyed every minute of her job. Mr. Tape was a most courteous and considerate employer, very precise and meticulous, and always ready with a word of praise for a task that was done well.

Jill had joined the firm when the tragic death of her mother and father in a railway accident had made her an orphan at the age of twenty-two with no other living relatives than an uncle, whom she had never seen, and an aunt whom she had, and had no particular wish to see again. She had, on the death of her parents, inherited a small income. It was a little less than three pounds a week, but, coupled with Mr. Tape's very generous salary, it enabled her to rent a small flat in Bloomsbury and live in a moderate degree of comfort. She was a tall, dark girl, with a good figure, whose chief asset was a pair of really lovely eyes of a large and liquid blue, through which she surveyed the world in general with a grave, slightly puzzled expression, as if she were mutely asking an eternal question, which was unusual and attractive.

She left the restaurant at twenty past six and took a taxi to Waterloo. It was a dark, unpleasant, November night and, although not actually raining, the thin mist which had come up with the setting of the sun made everything damp and clammy. She wondered, as she settled herself in the corner of an empty carriage of the Berrydale train, just what the important documents she was carrying consisted of. There were very few things concerning Mr. Tape's business which she did not know, but this was one of them. He had said nothing about them at all until he had made his request that afternoon.

Professor Locksley she had met on two occasions, both at Mr. Tape's offices. He was a thin, elderly man with the stooping back of the scholar, almost completely bald, and extremely short-sighted. He was an authority on Ancient Egypt and was engaged, so Mr. Tape had told her, on a monumental history of that fascinating country, the material for which he had been gathering during most of his life.

The train arrived at Berrydale Station exactly two minutes late, and with the exception of a man in a heavy overcoat, Jill was the only passenger to alight. The station was almost rural in its lack of amenities, which is not surprising considering that Berrydale itself has only very recently discarded the swaddling clothes of its village infancy and begun to grow up into an adolescent town.

Jill crossed the wooden footbridge over the line and gave up her ticket to a yawning porter at the narrow gate that formed the exit from the station on this side. It was very dark outside and, rather to her dismay, she found that the thin mist which had been scarcely more than a hint in London had, here, thickened into almost a fog. It was not so thick, however, that she couldn't see her way, and after pausing for a moment to get her bearings, she set off briskly along the road which Mr. Tape had described, determined to get her errand over as quickly as possible and get back into the cosy warmth of her flat before the fog settled down in earnest.

Mr. Tape's three minutes appeared to be somewhat of an understatement, for it was all of seven before she came to the roundabout which he had mentioned. There was a circular, stone-edged, grass plot in the centre from which an iron light standard reared up into the misty darkness and shed a feeble and bleary radiance. According to her employer's description, Hayford Avenue should begin on the opposite side in an almost direct line from where she was now standing.

She crossed over to the central grass patch and from thence to the opposite pavement. Two roads yawned blackly before her, the entrances to them like the apex of a triangle. She sought for some means of identifying Hayford Avenue, and presently found an oblong white board screwed to a wooden fence bearing the name in black leters. Number eighteen could not be very far down, she concluded, unless the numbers started from the other end, and according to Mr. Tape's rather metaphorical timing this was unlikely. She began to walk slowly along the curving road, looking for a number which would give her an idea of how they ran. The houses were fairly large and detached, set well back from the road in little forests of trees. The numbers, however, she discovered to her relief, were painted quite clearly on the gateposts, and presently she came to number eighteen. The gate was open and from what she could see of her surroundings as she entered the broad drive, the place had been thoroughly neglected. Weeds and patches of grass covered the gravel under her feet and grew in waist-high profusion everywhere else. She supposed that Professor Locksley was so wrapped up in the preparation of his Egyptian history that he had no interest in anything else. The drive led in a semi-circular sweep to a flight of steps under a creeper-covered porch. She mounted these and received the first shock of that eventful night.

The big front door was open. It wasn't fully open, but open about a foot, so that she could see a long strip of utter darkness inside. She hesitated, wondering whether she should push the door open wider and go in, and then, seeing a rusty iron knocker, she decided to make her presence known first. She knocked loudly, and the sound echoed and re-echoed from within so that her heart gave a little jump and almost stopped. There was no mistaking the reason for that hollow echo. The house was empty.

She stood, frowning in perplexity. It was quite absurd that the house should be empty. She had made no mistake. This was Hayford Avenue — she had verified that by the board at the entrance to the road — and this was number eighteen. The figures were plain enough on the gateposts. Not merely on one, but on both. She took the sealed envelope which Mr. Tape had given her from her handbag and, flicking on a lighter, looked at the address in the light of the feeble flame. No mistake there, either. 'Professor C. Locksley, 18 Hayford Avenue, Berrydale, Surrey,' clear and plain in neat typescript. Could Professor Locksley have suddenly moved for any reason? That seemed ridiculous. Mr. Tape would surely have known about it. Perhaps only part of the house was furnished? Perhaps the Professor had only recently moved in and had not settled yet . . . ?

Jill decided to explore further, and pushed open the front door. A smell of damp and decay came billowing out to her, and as she stepped across the threshold into the darkness of the hall her feet trod on bare boards. She flicked on the lighter again, and the tiny flame revealed a huge, empty hall, with the shadowy hint of a great staircase vanishing away into gloom. There was dust everywhere, dust and cobwebs . . . And quite suddenly she began to feel *afraid*. The hair on the back of her neck prickled, and a chill ripple ran up her spine. A wave of sheer panic gripped her and paralysed her limbs. There was something in the dust and darkness that was hideous and horrible, abominable and beastly . . .

She wanted to turn and run, but she could not move, and not for all the money in the world would she have turned her back on the cavernous gloom of that hall . . . And then she saw something in the shadow of the great staircase that was part of the shadow and yet was more tangible — a something that lay in the dust amid something that was not dust at all — something that spread slowly and sluggishly even while she looked — like a black *living* shadow . . .

3

'I don't mind it bein' cold, an' I don't mind rain,' remarked the grizzled-haired desk-sergeant, 'but I can't abide fog, an' that's a fact. There's something about a fog that's queer, if you understand what I mean, sir. It's sort o' unnatural-like.'

Mr. Budd nodded in agreement. He disliked fog, too. There *was* something uncanny about it. He had come to Berrydale Police Station to identify a man, long wanted by Scotland Yard for a series of frauds, who had been arrested that afternoon by an astute constable who had recognised him from the circulated description, and he was looking forward, without relish, to his journey back to London through the damp mist that was rapidly developing into a thick fog.

'Fog is the answer to the crook's prayer,' said the desk-sergeant, leaning forward on his elbows and preparing to enlarge upon his subject. 'I'll bet there's been more crimes done under cover of fog than at any other time. It's only natural. It's more like a blinkin' smoke screen when it gets properly thick. An' that's a thing what it wouldn't surprise me if they didn't start usin' soon — smoke screens . . . '

'Maybe they will,' grunted Mr. Budd, yawning. He was getting a little tired of the sergeant's efforts at entertaining conversation, and anxious to be gone. ''Ow long will this super'ntendent of yours be, d'you think?'

The desk-sergeant looked up at the big, round-faced clock on the wall of the charge room.

''E ought to be 'ere at any minute now, sir,' he replied. Since he had been saying the same thing at intervals for the past hour, Mr. Budd thought there was little reliance to be placed in his judgment.

'Well, I'll give 'im another fifteen minutes,' he said, 'an' then I'll 'ave to be goin' . . . ' He broke off abruptly as the door opened and a girl came hurriedly in. Her face was paper-white and she breathed heavily as though she had been running. In the sudden transition from the darkness outside to the comparative brightness of the charge room she blinked and swayed . . . Mr. Budd thought she was going to faint and, going to her, slipped a podgy hand under one arm.

'Take it easy, Miss,' he said, kindly. 'You look as if you'd 'ad a shock. What's the matter?'

Jill Hartley tried to recover her breath. She had run all the way from the ghastly thing in that dreadful house in Hayford Avenue — run desperately, scarcely knowing where she ran, until the blue lamp shining through the fog had told her . . .

'Here,' went on the big superintendent, guiding her over to a chair, 'you sit yourself down until you get yer breath back, and then you can tell us all about it. What was it? Somebody molest yer, was it?'

She shook her head.

'No . . . ' she gasped with difficulty. 'It was a dead man . . . '

Mr. Budd's genial expression changed suddenly.

'A dead man, Miss?' he said, sharply. 'Where?'

'In . . . the . . . empty house,' she answered, jerkily. 'By . . . the staircase in the . . . hall. There was . . . a lot of . . . blood.'

'Which house was this, Miss?' put in the desk-sergeant, who had been listening with open-mouthed interest.

'Hayford Avenue . . . ' said Jill. She was rapidly recovering her breath and was able to speak more coherently. 'Professor Locksley's house — number eighteen . . . '

'Professor Locksley's house?' repeated Mr. Budd in in puzzled tone. 'I thought you said it was an *empty* 'ouse, Miss . . . ?'

'It *was* empty,' she answered quickly. 'But it shouldn't have been. Professor Locksley should have been living there.'

'And you found a dead man in the 'all?' asked the stout superintendent.

'Yes,' she said with a shiver. 'In a pool of . . . of blood. It was horrible . . . '

Mr. Budd looked sleepily across at the desk-sergeant.

'I think I'd better look inter this,' he

18

said, slowly. 'I'll take a constable with me . . . ' He turned to the girl. 'I've got my car outside, Miss,' he murmured. 'Could you show me this empty house where you found the dead man?'

Jill nodded.

'Yes,' she said. 'I can show you. Only don't ask me to go in . . . I couldn't face that dreadful thing again . . . '

'Don't you worry about anythin', Miss,' said Mr. Budd, soothingly. 'Just you leave all the worryin' ter me, an' while we're on the way to this empty house you can tell me how you come to be there.'

The desk-sergeant had sent for a constable, and when the man arrived, Mr. Budd accompanied him and the girl to where he had left his dilapidated little car.

'Now, Miss,' he said, when he had squeezed his enormous bulk behind the wheel and Jill had taken the seat beside him, with the constable occupying the back: 'Just you tell me all about it.'

She told him all about it while he drove through the murky fog in the direction of Hayford Avenue.

'Interestin' and peculiar,' murmured

the big man. 'You go to deliver some documents ter this Professor Locksley an' yer find the 'ouse empty an' a dead man in the hall . . . '

'Excuse me, sir,' the voice of the constable broke in. 'But the house wasn't empty yesterday, sir.'

'Oh, it wasn't, eh?' said Mr. Budd. 'H'm. Are you sure of that?'

'Yes, sir, quite sure,' replied the man. 'You see, it happens to be on my beat . . . '

'Queer,' said Mr. Budd. 'Very queer. The 'ouse wasn't empty yesterday an' now it's empty an' full o' dust an' cobwebs. You sure it wasn't the *wrong* house, you went to, Miss?'

'It was Eighteen Hayford Avenue that I went to,' declared Jill. 'I saw the name at the end of the road and the number on the gateposts.'

'And that house wasn't empty yesterday, sir,' put in the constable, 'as sure as I'm a-sittin' 'ere.'

'Very queer,' remarked Mr. Budd, thoughtfully. 'There's somethin' wrong somewhere. A 'ouse can't get full o' dust an' cobwebs in a single night . . . Which way do we go now?' They had reached the roundabout and he slowed down, peering through the thickening mist.

'Round to the right, an' the first on the left,' said the constable. 'That's 'Ayford Avenue.'

Mr. Budd obeyed the direction. The car half-circled the central green patch and swung into the yawning mouth of a road to the left. Here the big man brought it to a halt. 'Is this the place, Miss?' he asked.

Jill stared out through the dark mist.

'Yes,' she said. 'Yes, I think so.'

'Better make sure,' said Mr. Budd. 'Just step out, will you, an' have a look at the name-plate . . . '

'There's no doubt about it, sir,' said the constable, to whom the request had been addressed, but he went all the same. He was back in a few seconds.

''Ayford Avenue,' he said, triumphantly. 'I was sure there weren't no mistake. Number eighteen's just along on the left . . . '

Mr. Budd drove forward slowly, keeping close in to the kerb. Presently the constable called out to him to stop.

'This should be about it, sir,' he said.

'All right, we'll get out,' grunted the big man, pulling up. Jill and the constable got out, and Mr. Budd followed laboriously.

'Here you are, sir,' said the constable, 'I thought I weren't far out. This is eighteen.' He pointed to the numbers, plainly visible on a pair of gateposts, but Jill, after one look, stopped and shook her head.

'That's not the place,' she declared.

'That's number eighteen, Miss,' said the policeman, 'an' this is 'Ayford Avenue . . . '

'I don't care,' said Jill, emphatically. 'That is *not* the house I came to earlier tonight!'

4

Mr. Budd scratched his fleshy chin dubiously. It suddenly occurred to him that this girl might suffer from delusions. Except for the obvious effect of shock, she had appeared normal enough, but one never knew . . .

'You're absolutely sure this is Hayford Avenue?' he said to the constable. The man was absolutely sure. He had seen the name written up on the fence at the end of the road, and besides, he knew the neighbourhood well . . .

'Could you 'ave made a mistake, Miss?' suggested the big detective. 'Maybe it wasn't 'Ayford Avenue that you went to . . . ?'

But Jill was as emphatic as the policeman. She had taken particular care to make sure, because she had never been to Berrydale before.

Mr. Budd sighed gently.

'Well,' he remarked, 'you say this

Professor What's-his-Name lives at Eighteen Hayford Avenue? Let's go and see. That'll prove it one way or the other.'

He led the way ponderously over to the gate, and up the drive, followed by the bewildered Jill and the stolid constable. There was not the slightest doubt that this was *not* the house that she had visited before. The approach was neat, the bushes trim, and the flowerbeds carefully tended. There was no sign of the neglect of that other garden. From what she could see of it in the gloom and mist, it was a different place altogether . . .

Mr. Budd mounted the steps before the large, black-painted front door and knocked. There was a short pause, and then they heard a faint footfall. The door was opened and, silhouetted against the soft glow of light that illumined the big hall, stood an elderly woman dressed in black silk.

'Good evenin', Ma'am,' said Mr. Budd. 'Does Professor Locksley live 'ere?'

'Yes, sir,' said the woman. 'Did you wish to see him?'

'Is this Eighteen Hayford Avenue?' put

in Jill quickly, and the woman inclined her head.

Mr. Budd grunted. He was satisfied now that the girl had either made a mistake or that she very definitely suffered from delusions. This house, judging from what he could see of the hall, was beautifully furnished, and looked as though it had been so for a long time. There was no sign of dust or cobwebs, or of blood and dead men . . .

'Could I see Professor Locksley?' said Jill, in a voice that betrayed her complete and utter astonishment. 'I have a letter for him from Mr. Tape, of Messrs . . . '

'Oh yes, Miss,' said the woman, instantly. 'Professor Locksley has been expecting you. Will you come in, please?'

'Now, you see, Miss,' said Mr. Budd. 'You must 'ave imagined all this business of . . . '

'I did nothing of the sort,' said Jill, sharply. 'I saw the man lying dead in that horrible dusty hall. You come in with me. I'm going to ask Professor Locksley about it and see what he says.'

Mr. Budd yawned wearily, and turned

to the constable.

'You wait 'ere, What's-yer-name,' he said.

'Nutts,' replied the constable.

'Eh!' said the big man, under the momentary impression that the man was being rude.

'Nutts, sir,' explained the policeman. 'That's my name.'

'Oh, I see,' grunted Mr. Budd. 'Well, you wait. I'm goin' ter get to the bottom of this business.'

The woman, evidently a superior servant, probably the housekeeper, who had been waiting patiently, and with a certain amount of astonishment, while this interchange had been going on, led the way up the broad, heavily carpeted stairs, to the first floor, and knocked at a closed door.

'Come in, come in,' called a faint voice, impatiently. 'What do you want?'

'The young lady you were expecting is here, sir,' said the housekeeper, opening the door.

'Oh . . . well, bring her in,' snapped the impatient voice, and the woman ushered

Jill into a large room crammed with books and relics of ancient Egypt. Behind a huge, untidy writing table sat a lean, bald-headed man, wearing large, horn-rimmed glasses. He rose as they entered and revealed that he was very tall, with a pronounced stoop. What Jill had expected she would have found difficulty in expressing in words, but this was undoubtedly Professor Cedric Locksley.

'Come in, Miss Hartley, come in,' said Professor Locksley, in a high, slightly querulous voice. 'Mr. Tape telephoned me that you would be coming.' He looked beyond her at Mr. Budd, and his rather bushy eyebrows, which was the only hair visible about him, rose interrogatively.

'I'm a police officer from Scotland Yard, sir,' Mr. Budd introduced himself. 'This lady 'as had rather an unpleasant experience, from what she tells me . . . '

'An unpleasant experience?' repeated Locksley, and the bushy eyebrows descended sharply. 'You haven't lost the — the documents that Tape . . . ?'

'No, no,' said Jill, hastily. 'I have them here.'

She took the sealed envelope from her bag and gave it to him. Locksley took it in his lean hands and there was relief on his face.

'Mr. Tape would like a receipt,' said Jill.

'Yes, yes. Of course, of course,' said Professor Locksley, impatiently. 'I will go through these and give you one. What was this 'experience' to which you referred — er — superintendent?'

Mr. Budd cleared his throat.

'I think the young lady 'd better tell you 'erself, sir,' he answered.

Jill was quite ready to do that, and did so, with a burst of graphic detail. Professor Locksley listened with a puzzled frown on his long face.

'It would appear that you must have gone to the wrong house,' he remarked, when she had finished.

'But how could I?' protested Jill. 'I read the name — Hayford Avenue — clearly. It was in black letters on white, and the number, eighteen, was quite large. I couldn't have made a mistake . . . '

'Well, this is the only Eighteen Hayford Avenue in Berrydale,' said Locksley, with a faint smile. 'And there is nothing very empty about *this* house. In fact,' he added, with a touch of humour that was rather unexpected, 'it is getting so full that I have difficulty in finding room for everything. My housekeeper, Mrs. Moule, will assure you that there is neither dust nor cobwebs, and I can vouch for the fact that there arc no dead men, with the exception of those mummies.' He waved his hand towards a large glass case that stood in one corner.

'Well, there *was* a house, and a dead man, too,' said Jill, who in spite of her bewilderment was getting a little annoyed. 'I saw both and I wasn't imagining it . . . '

'So you must have made a mistake, Miss,' said Mr. Budd.

'There's another road that runs almost parallel with this,' said Professor Locksley, rubbing his chin thoughtfully. 'Court Road, it's called . . . '

'How could I have mistaken Court Road for Hayford Avenue?' demanded Jill. 'The names are not even alike . . . '

'Do you happen to know, sir, if there's an empty 'ouse in Court Road?' asked

Mr. Budd, and Locksley shook his bald head.

'I'm afraid I don't,' he replied. 'I know very little about the neighbourhood. I seldom go out, and when I do, it is mostly to attend lectures or meetings . . . '

'Well, it's very easily put to the test,' broke in Jill. 'Let's find Number Eighteen Court Road and see . . . '

'I think that is a very good suggestion,' said Professor Locksley. 'Come back here afterwards, Miss Hartley, and I will give you the receipt for Mr. Tape.'

5

Once more they were out in the damp mist, which had thickened appreciably, so that now it was difficult to see more than a few yards ahead. Mr. Budd wondered, if it continued to thicken, how he was going to grope his way home to Streatham, and decided that in that event it would be preferable to spend the night at the police station. Constable Nutts had agreed to lead the way to Court Road, which was only a few yards from the entrance to Hayford Avenue, and presently they found themselves walking along a road that was very similar to the one they had just left. The big man had insisted on examining the name plates at the beginning of each road, and found that although they were the same in size and everything but the names, these were quite unmistakable. It seemed impossible that Jill Hartley, searching for the specified Hayford Avenue, could have made a mistake, even in the swirling mist and darkness. In a little while they came to a gatepost bearing the number eighteen, and immediately Jill uttered an exclamation.

'This is the place!' she cried. 'This is where I came . . . '

'An' this is eighteen *Court Road*, Miss,' murmured Mr. Budd. 'So you see you must've made a mistake, after all . . . '

'I can't imagine how,' said the girl, in complete bewilderment. 'I'm absolutely certain the board at the end said Hayford Avene. I simply *couldn't* have been mistaken.'

Mr. Budd was beginning to think that she couldn't, either. And if she hadn't, then something very queer had been going on in that neighbourhood under cover of the darkness and the mist. For, if Jill Hartley had *not* been mistaken, if she had actually read 'Hayford Avenue' where 'Court Road' should have been, and very definitely *was*, then somebody must, for their own purposes, have changed the signs, or covered them with others, exchanging the name of one road for the other.

'Come along,' he said. 'I'm beginnin' ter believe in this dead man of yours, Miss. Put yer light on, Nutts, an' lead the way.'

The policeman unhitched his lantern and threw a bright beam up the neglected driveway. As he advanced toward the house. Mr. Budd and Jill followed him, the former keeping his sleepy-looking eyes on the ground. The dark mass of the porch loomed up and then the deep shadows fled before the light of the constable's lantern. The door was wide open, as Jill had left it when she had fled in panic from the horror of the hall, and, as Nutts was about to cross the threshold, Mr. Budd called to him gently.

'Don't you go no further,' he said. 'Just you stay where you are an' shine yer light. You stay with 'im, Miss.'

'I wouldn't go in there again for . . . for anything,' declared Jill fervently. 'He . . . it . . . was . . . over . . . beside the staircase.'

The big man nodded, lumbered up the steps and stood for a moment beside the constable peering into the great hall.

'Throw yer light down — on the floor,' he ordered, and, when the constable obeyed, he saw in the dust several tracks of footprints. The girl's small, high-heeled shoes were easily distinguishable and there were two other sets of distinctive prints — a large, broad-soled shoe and a narrow, lighter one. Mr. Budd entered the hall carefully, taking every precaution not to obliterate any of the prints in the dust. At a word, the interested policeman raised his light so that it flooded the staircase, and the stout superintendent caught his breath as he saw the sprawling figure that huddled beside the bottom stair. Keeping close to the wall, he sidled over to it and bent down. It was a man — or had been, for there was no doubt that he was dead. The top of his head had been battered to pulp, and from these wounds the blood had flowed to form the dusty pool in which he lay . . .

Mr. Budd remained for a long minute staring intently at the hideous sight, and then he slowly straightened up. This was murder, and the usual routine would have to be set in motion. He sighed wearily.

There was no need to worry any longer how he was going to get home. It looked as though he would be busy for the greater part of the night with this . . .

'Go to the nearest police box an' telephone the 'nick',' he said to the constable. 'Tell 'em there's been a murder at Eighteen Court Road and ask 'em to send the Divisional Surgeon, an' an ambulance, an' then come back 'ere. Leave yer lamp.'

The constable turned away, and Mr. Budd rejoined Jill. 'When 'e comes back,' he said, ''e can take you round to this Professor feller's and stay there with yer until I'm through with this little packet . . . '

'Can't I go home,' she asked.

'I'm afraid you can't, Miss,' said Mr. Budd, pushing his hat to the back of his head and rubbing his brow. 'Not for a bit, anyhow. Yer see, this is murder, an' you made the discovery . . . '

'But I don't know anything more than I've told you,' she said.

'All the same, we've got to foller routine,' said the big man. How could he tell her that he had only her word that she knew nothing more than she had said? That it was impossible to let her go until they had found out a great deal more about her . . . ? But Jill did not work in a lawyer's office for nothing, and she guessed what was passing in his mind.

'Oh, I see,' she said, and smiled — that attractive smile that usually wreaked havoc in the male breast. 'I suppose I'm the principal suspect?'

'Well, I wouldn't exac'ly say that, Miss,' said Mr. Budd with a great deal of truth.

'But that's what you're thinking,' said Jill. 'You're wasting your time over me. I don't know anything about this horrible business . . . '

'I'm sure you don't, Miss,' said the big man, soothingly. 'But a p'lice investigation 'as got to be conducted accordin' to rule, you see, an' what I think, an' what I don't think, don't really matter.'

'I know,' said Jill. 'But I'm very tired and cold, and I would like to go home as soon as possible. I'm sure Professor Locksley would vouch for my good character and, of course, Mr. Tape of

Messrs. Tape, Redman and Tape, of Lincoln's Inn. You could telephone him . . .'

Mr. Budd promised her that he would let her go as soon as he possibly could, and they waited in the cold porch for the return of the constable. He came in a few minutes to say that an inspector, a sergeant, and the police doctor would arrive shortly.

'Take this young lady round to Professor Locksley's and stay there until I come,' said Mr. Budd, and Jill departed with the policeman, thankful, at any rate, to get away from the horrible house and its silent occupant.

Left to himself, Mr. Budd produced a thin, black cigar from an inner pocket, bit off the end, and lit it, blowing out a cloud of acrid, poisonous smoke with a sigh of satisfaction.

It was three parts consumed before he heard the sound of a car approaching. It drew up outside the gate and a small group of men materialised out of the mist; an inspector, a sergeant, a constable, a man with a large suitcase, and another carrying a little black bag which stamped him as the police doctor. Mr. Budd gave the inspector, who introduced himself as Peel, a brief account of the circumstances relating to the discovery, and then the routine investigation into wilful murder began. The doctor made his examination and reported that the man had been dead for at least two hours. He had died from heavy and repeated blows on the head delivered by a blunt instrument wielded with a great deal of strength . . .

'Considerable superficies . . . posterior part of the cranium . . . extensive fractures . . . hæmorrhagic effusion into the cortex . . . ' The doctor reeled off a string of technical phrases. When he had finished, the man with the suitcase took over. From the suitcase he produced a large camera and flashlight apparatus. Photographs of the hall, the footprints in the dust, and of the corpse were taken, and when this had been completed, Mr. Budd made a search of the body. The dead man was small and neatly made. His face was clean-shaven and the skin was olive-hued. With his dark hair and brows, he had the appearance of a foreigner. His clothes were good, and he was wearing a thick and heavy overcoat of Harris tweed. The big man, assisted by the inspector, went carefully through his pockets. There was not very much worthy of note. A gold watch and chain with a bunch of queerly designed seals attached; a wallet of worn crocodile skin containing eight pounds in notes and a book of stamps; two Yale keys on a steel ring; a fountain pen, and a small quantity of silver and copper money. And that was all. There was nothing in the way of letter or document to show who the man was or anything about him. Mr. Budd rose, red in the face and breathing heavily from his exertions.

'Well, that's that!' he grunted. 'The first thin' we've to do is ter find out his identity. He may as well be taken away now.'

A stretcher was brought in from the ambulance and the dead man lifted on to it. As they moved him, Mr. Budd caught sight of a scrap of paper that had been hidden under the body. It was soaked with blood, and he picked it up delicately

by one corner. Two words were decipher-
able in ink . . . 'Seven Lamps . . . ' but
they conveyed nothing to the stout
superintendent. He took out his pocketbook and put the gruesome and still
damp little relic carefully away in an old
envelope. Many things were to happen
before he realised that in those two words
lay the key to the strange affair, one scene
of which had been staged that misty night
in the empty house in Court Road.

6

Jill Hartley sipped the hot coffee which Mrs. Moule, at Professor Locksley's request, had made for her. It helped to drive away the chill which seemed to have crept into her very bones, and did something to remove the devitalising effect of the shock she had sustained. Locksley watched her gravely from behind the big writing-table, his thin hands fumbling nervously with a pencil.

'I don't think you had better attempt to travel back to London tonight, Miss Hartley,' he remarked, after a long silence. 'The fog is getting thicker and there will probably be a delay in the trains, even if they continue to run at all. My housekeeper will be able to supply you with anything you need . . . '

'It's very kind of you,' said Jill, 'but . . . '

'I shall listen to no 'buts',' interrupted the Professor. 'You will stay here. I shall instruct Mrs. Moule to that effect. After all, you experienced this unpleasantness and — er — inconvenience on my behalf, and the offer of hospitality on such an inclement night is the least I can do. I shall telephone Tape in the morning and explain . . . '

'Mr. Tape is not expecting me until after lunch,' said Jill. 'He said I could have the morning off . . . '

'Then everything is settled,' said Locksley. 'You will remain.' He pressed a bell on his desk, and after a few seconds' delay, Mrs. Moule put in an appearance.

'Miss Hartley will be staying the night,' he said. 'I'm sure you will be able to — er — make her comfortable?'

'Certainly, sir,' said the woman, instantly. 'I will put a fire and make up the bed in the spare room . . . '

'I don't want to be a lot of trouble . . . ' began Jill.

'It will be no trouble at all, Miss,' asserted the housekeeper, firmly. 'I will attend to it at once.'

Jill refrained from further argument. She had been looking forward with dread to the cold and cheerless journey back, and she welcomed the proposal of staying in this warm, well-ordered house.

'I confess,' said Professor Locksley, when the housekeeper had gone, 'to a very great interest in this mysterious business. I cannot understand how you can have come to make a mistake between this road and Court Road in the first place, but it is evident that you did, and so stumbled upon this appalling discovery.'

'I'm still puzzled,' said Jill, snuggling back into the easy chair. 'I would be prepared to swear in a court of law that what I read on that board was Hayford Avenue.'

'Which goes to prove,' said Locksley, with a little smile, 'how even the most apparently reliable witness can be wrong . . . '

'But I'm sure I wasn't wrong,' declared the girl. 'I couldn't have been wrong. There is no resemblance at all between the two names. How could I have imagined that what I saw was Hayford Avenue?'

Professor Locksley shook his high, bald head slowly.

'The mind plays some strange tricks at times,' he said, meditatively. 'We see something that we want, or expect, to see, although the actual thing we are looking at is different. I believe something of the sort must have happened to you tonight.'

Jill was not at all impressed with this explanation. After all, *she* was the one who had seen that board, and the recollection of it was so vivid that she refused to believe that she had dragged it up from some queer hinterland of the mind. Before she could reply, however, there came a loud knock on the door, and it burst open to admit an unruly-haired, freckled-faced young man in a shabby raincoat.

'Hello, Uncle!' cried the newcomer, boisterously. 'What's the idea of the peeler in the hall, eh? Has there been a burglary, a murder, or have they pinched you for unpaid income tax . . . ?' He caught sight of Jill and stopped abruptly. 'Oh . . . I didn't know you had a visitor . . . '

'It wouldn't have made any difference if you had, I suppose?' grunted Professor Locksley. 'Miss Hartley, this is my nephew, Richard Wayland. 'A poor thing, but, unfortunately, mine own'.'

'How do you do, Miss Hartley?' greeted Mr. Wayland, with a broad grin. 'I never knew that Uncle Cedric was acquainted with anything so attractive. He's certainly stepping out in his old age . . . '

Jill felt herself reddening at this blatant compliment, and was annoyed.

'That will be quite enough of *that*, Richard,' said his Uncle, severely. 'You can reserve that kind of talk for your rather low acquaintances. I thought you weren't coming back until late?'

'She never turned up,' replied Richard, completely unabashed. 'The fog, I suppose. Pity, she was both young and comely, and I never even got her telephone number. Another budding romance shattered. What's the rozzer doing downstairs?'

'If you are referring to the constable,' said Professor Locksley, 'he is here to look after Miss Hartley . . . '

'Good Lord!' exclaimed his nephew, raising his eyebrows. 'What have you been doing, eh? Or did you bring him with you, knowing that any young and innocent girl would require police protection when visiting my Uncle? He's always been a notorious roué, but we have tried to keep the dread secret for the sake of the family name . . . '

'Will you stop talking nonsense?' broke in his Uncle, sharply. 'There has been serious trouble in the neighbourhood tonight. A man has been murdered . . . '

'A murder? Phew!' Richard Wayland whistled softly. 'Well, that offers some compensation for the non-appearance of the beauteous blonde. Why did you murder a man, Miss Hartley?'

'I didn't,' protested Jill, indignantly. 'I know nothing about it at all. I only found the body . . . '

'Well, that's something,' said Richard. '*I* never find bodies, at least, not dead ones. I'll admit the blonde had rather a good line in that direction . . . '

'We have no wish to hear about it,'

46

snapped Professor Locksley. 'If you can't behave yourself, you'd better go to bed.'

'No fear,' said Richard. 'I wouldn't be out of this for anything. Where did you find the gruesome remains?' He cocked an interrogative eye at Jill.

'If you can keep quiet long enough to listen,' said Professor Locksley, 'I'll tell you the circumstances, so far as we know them.' Concisely and methodically he proceeded to do so, and Richard listened in unexpected silence.

'H'm, queer business,' he commented at the end of the recital. 'I suppose they're keeping an eye on you because they're not quite sure how much you do know, eh?'

Jill nodded.

'I believe that is the idea,' she said.

'Quite ridiculous, of course,' remarked Professor Locksley, 'but I suppose the police have to exercise every precaution in a serious matter like this.'

'I don't see how you could have made a mistake,' said Richard, frowning, and for the moment quite serious. 'Over the names of the two roads, I mean. It seems incredible to me . . . '

'Are you suggesting that I'm lying, Mr. Wayland?' asked Jill, calmly.

'Good Lord, no!' exclaimed Richard. 'I'm merely suggesting that there was some fishy business somewhere. It looks to me as if the murderer had done something to those name plates — switched them over or something like that — so as to lure this unfortunate chap to the empty house . . . '

'Don't be absurd, Richard,' said Locksley testily. 'If that were the case, this unknown man who was murdered must have thought he was coming here . . . '

'Yes, that's true,' murmured Richard, making a grimace and wrinkling his nose 'Well, perhaps he *was* coming here?'

'I wasn't expecting anybody,' said Locksley.

'Then it must have been somebody you *didn't* expect,' said Richard. 'Look here, Uncle, you often have valuable specimens brought here, don't you? Ancient relics, old papyri?' He waved his hand round the crowded room. 'Why shouldn't this man have been bringing something of the sort?

Something very valuable that he hoped to sell to you?'

'Well, I suppose it's possible,' admitted Professor Locksley doubtfully, passing a thin hand over his naked crown. 'You're suggesting that this man was killed for something valuable he was bringing to me?'

'It's an idea, anyway,' said Richard. 'If the murderer knew about it, and had played monkey tricks with the names of the roads, he would go to Eighteen Court Road, the *empty house*, thinking he was coming here — the same as Miss Hartley did ... Look here, haven't you got another name? Miss Hartley's a hell of a mouthful ...'

'Jill,' she said without thinking.

'Jill,' said Richard. 'That's better ... pretty name, too. Well, Jill, don't you agree that it might have happened that way?'

'I'd rather believe that than that I made a mistake,' said Jill. 'The training of a solicitor's office is not conducive to mistakes.'

'Is that what you do?' said Richard,

with great interest. 'I must remember that. When I get into a scrape I shall come to you to get me out . . .'

'Miss Hartley works for Mr. Tape,' said Professor Locksley. 'I omitted to mention that. You know there's something in what you say, Richard.'

'There's always something in what I say,' remarked his nephew. He produced a packet of Players and held it out. 'Cigarette, Jill?'

She took one and he adroitly flicked a lighter into flame and lit it for her.

'Not always something of sense,' retorted his uncle. 'Your conversational powers are usually limited to two subjects, yourself and women . . .'

'Hush!' exclaimed Richard in mock alarm. 'You'll be giving Jill a bad impression of me.' He grinned at the girl, lit a cigarette, and proceeded to blow a rapid succession of rings towards the ceiling.

'I must apologise for my nephew,' said Professor Locksley gravely, but with a suspicion of a twinkle in his eyes. 'I have been given to understand that as a very small child he fell out of his pram on to his head, and has never entirely recovered from the consequences.'

'In that case he deserves more pity than blame,' remarked Jill.

'You can pity me as much as you like,' said Richard. 'Remember what the poet said? 'Pity is akin to love.' Until I met you, I was a gentleman who preferred blondes.'

Again Jill felt herself reddening, and embarrassment engendered her retort.

'But not a gentleman whom blondes prefer, apparently,' she said sweetly. 'At least, judging from your experience this evening.'

'*Touché!*' cried Richard, with great delight. 'The retort discourteous! You are a lady of infinite jest! I can only thank whatever gods were responsible that I was not otherwise engaged this evening and so have experienced the inestimable privilege and joy of meeting you. What are you doing tomorrow evening? How about dinner and a spot of dancing . . . ?'

'Really, Richard!' protested his scandalised Uncle. 'I think you are going a little too far . . . '

'I always behave with perfect decorum,' said Richard. 'Even in a taxi! I am known to the chorus girls' union as the perfect gent . . . '

'I'm afraid I can't accept your kind invitation,' said Jill. 'I don't belong to the union you mention and, therefore, your behaviour might not apply in my case.'

Mrs. Moule came in at that moment to state that the room was ready.

'Are you staying?' asked Richard. 'Oh, that's fine! I shall renew my invitation at breakfast . . . '

'You can save your breath,' retorted Jill. 'You'll only get the same answer.'

'Turned down twice in one evening,' sighed Richard, shaking his head. 'I must be losing my grip . . . '

'And a very good thing, too,' remarked his Uncle.

'It's high time you stopped all this frivolous nonsense and began to take life seriously . . . Come in.'

It was the housekeeper again, to announce that Superintendent Budd was downstairs and would like to see Miss Hartley.

'Show him up here,' ordered Professor Locksley.

'It looks as if you are going to spend tomorrow in a cold and cheerless prison cell instead of dancing with me,' said Richard.

'It would be preferable,' retorted Jill, icily, and before he could think of a suitable reply, the housekeeper ushered in the portly figure of Mr. Budd.

6

'I shan't 'ave to trouble you again tonight, Miss,' said the big man, 'but I thought, maybe, you'd like to see these. We found 'em hidden in some bushes.'

He produced from under his arm two narrow strips of thin plywood. They had been painted a dirty white, and on them in black letters were the words: 'Hayford Avenue' and 'Court Road'. They were facsimiles in every detail of the genuine name plates.

'You didn't make no mistake, Miss,' said Mr. Budd. 'You see these small 'ooks at the back of these? That's how they was hung over the real ones. With these in place, Hayford Avenue became Court Road, an' Court Road 'Ayford Avenue. Simple but clever.'

'There you are!' exclaimed Richard, triumphantly. 'That proves what I was saying just now.'

Mr. Budd looked at him with sleepy-eyed interest.

'What *was* you sayin', sir?' he asked.

Richard repeated his theory with great gusto.

'H'm, remarked the superintendent, when he concluded. 'I think you're pretty near the truth, sir. Which means that this feller who was killed was comin' here, an' somebody wanted to stop 'im.' He rubbed his fleshy chin gently.

'Who was this man?' asked Professor Locksley. 'The man who was murdered?'

'I'd like to be able to tell you,' replied Mr. Budd. 'It 'ud be a great help if I knew that, sir. But there was nuthin' on him to give us a clue to his identity. From his appearance he looked like some kind of foreigner, but that's about all I can say at present. You wasn't expectin' anybody like that?'

Locksley shook his head.

'No, Superintendent,' he answered. 'With the exception of Miss Hartley, I wasn't expecting anybody.'

'Well, there's not much doubt that he was comin' 'ere to see you, sir,' said Mr. Budd. 'There'd've been no point in the name-changing business otherwise. Maybe you'd recognise 'im if you saw 'im? P'raps you'd come along first thing in the mornin' and take a look at 'im, sir?'

Professor Locksley regarded the suggestion with obvious distaste, but reluctantly promised that he would.

'Was there nothing on the body at all to suggest his identity?' said Richard.

'No, sir,' replied Mr. Budd.

'That's rather queer, isn't it?'

'Well, yes, sir,' admitted the big man. 'In a way it is. In my opinion the murderer took away with 'im anythin' there may have been.'

'So as to prevent his identity being discovered?'

'So as to delay it,' corrected Mr. Budd. 'We shall find out who 'e was, sooner or later, but the longer we take the more chance there is for the killer to get away.' He suddenly recollected the bloodstained scrap of paper he had found under the body. 'There was one thin', but it don't mean anythin' to me. When we lifted him to put 'im on the stretcher there was a bit of paper with two words on it underneath 'im. 'Seven Lamps', that's all.'

'Seven Lamps,' repeated Professor Locksley, and his bushy brows came down over his eyes. 'Seven Lamps' . . . His long face changed suddenly from thoughtfulness to an expression of incredulity. Mr. Budd, whose apparently sleepy eyes missed nothing, saw the change of expression.

'Does it mean anything to you, sir?' he asked.

'I don't know . . . I don't know,' murmured Locksley, rubbing his high forehead. 'If it should refer to what I think, it's . . . it's . . . ' He got up abruptly and walked over to a section of the many bookshelves that lined the room. Peering along a laden shelf, he selected an ancient volume bound in a queer kind of vellum. Carrying it back to his desk, he reseated himself, adjusted his spectacles, and turned the aged yellow pages slowly and tenderly.

'This,' he explained, 'is a very rare book. There is, to my knowledge, no other copy in existence . . . '

'What is it?' asked Jill.

'It is a translation of the Holling Papyrus in manuscript,' said Professor Locksley, continuing to turn the pages reverently. 'Ah, here we are. Listen to this . . . ' He began to read from the page in front of him: ' . . . 'in the pyramid was a chamber and within the chamber a second chamber and within the second chamber was a third chamber, and the third chamber was lined with gold. In the walls of the third chamber were seven niches and in the first niche was a lamp of alabaster and in the second a lamp of copper and in the third a lamp of bronze and in the fourth a lamp of brass and in the fifth a lamp of iron and in the sixth a lamp of silver and in the seventh a lamp of gold, and each one of these seven lamps was dedicated to a god and possesses the powers of that god for the *Khu* dwells therein. That of Osiris dwells in the lamp of alabaster, that of Thoth in the lamp of copper; that of Anubis in the lamp of bronze, that of Horus in the lamp of brass; that of Set in the lamp of iron; that of Isis in the lamp of silver, and that of Ra in the lamp of gold. And the chamber is guarded by serpents and many noxious reptiles, but he who knows the Words of Power may pass unscathed therein and learn the secrets of Heaven and Earth, for to him who shall understand, the Lamps of the Gods are all powerful' . . . '

Professor Locksley ceased reading and looked up.

'You think that was what was meant by the seven lamps, sir?' asked Mr. Budd.

The old man shook his head.

'I don't know,' he anwered slowly. 'It was a mere suggestion . . . it suddenly occurred to me.'

'These lamps 'ud be very valuable, I suppose?' remarked Mr. Budd, thoughtfully.

'Of incalculable value . . . if they were ever found,' said Professor Locksley. 'To my knowledge they never have been found. There is even some doubt that they ever existed . . . this was written five thousand years ago . . . '

The big man pursed his thick lips.

'Five thousand years,' he murmured. 'That's a long time, sir — a mighty long time. But relics have bin found as old as that, 'aven't they, sir?'

'Oh, yes,' agreed Locksley. He got up, took the book, and, walking over to the bookcase, replaced it carefully on the shelf. 'I can only hope that these lamps have *not* been found,' he said, gravely tapping the bookcase with his lean fingers.

'Why, sir?' asked Mr. Budd.

'Because,' answered Professor Locksley, coming out of the shadow into the light of the desk lamp, 'they would endow the person who possessed them, if he knew how to use them, with unlimited power — such a power for good, or evil, as the world has never known.'

PART TWO

KARINA

1

The house stood on the fringe of Wimbledon Common, facing the delicate tracery of a forest of silver birches, invisible, now, in the clammy white mist that swirled and eddied round them and lay thickly in the hollows. It was an old house of Georgian architecture, with an imposing façade, half covered by a growth of ivy, set amid tangled shrubberies and untrimmed lawns and flowerbeds running wild with weeds. Its long line of shuttered windows stared, blank and lightless, at the damp unpleasantness of the night, but within, shaded lamps of unusual but beautiful design shed a soft glow on polished floors and rare carpets; on rich hangings and pictures, statuettes and vases, and furniture which time had mellowed and ripened and enriched.

In a large, high-ceilinged room opening off the entrance hall, a girl lay on a gold-covered settee, smoking a cigarette through a long carved jade holder, and reading a book. She was slim and lovely, with a mass of loose hair of a deep chestnut colour, caught back on one side of her white forehead by a gold and emerald ornament. The house frock of white crêpe de chine which she wore showed every curve and line of her exquisite figure, and on her small feet were a pair of gold sandals, fastened with buckles, in which two green stones sparkled and scintillated in the light from the golden lamp that hung from slender chains above her head. The entire room was a colour scheme of gold and green and black. A black carpet of thick, soft pile covered the floor, and the walls were draped with heavy silken hangings of eau de nil green, looped back here and there to reveal niches in which stood statuettes in black basalt of the gods of ancient Egypt. The furniture was of ebony, inlaid with gold and jade, and wonderfully carved. There were no pictures of the ordinary kind, but in the centre of each wall hung framed copies, beautifully executed, of papyri depicting scenes from the Egyptian Ritual of the Dead. The whole effect was bizarre and, to Western eyes, a trifle ornate. But the girl who lay upon the golden settee blent with her surroundings perfectly. Her complexion was of the hue of a soft tan with a dusky reddish tinge on the high cheek bones, and the long, dark silken lashes shadowed a pair of eyes that were slightly slanted and almond-shaped. Her features were small and delicately formed and her mouth was the colour of a ripe pomegranate. She was exotic and suggested in some indefinable way the hot glare of an Eastern sun, arid, burning sands, and all the colour and pageantry of the Orient.

The muted, musical chimes of a clock broke the utter silence of the room, and she laid down her book to listen. It chimed the quarters and then, in a deeper tone, struck twice. Coincident with the second note, the door opened and an old man came softly into the room. His hair was snow white and his eyes were deeply sunken in his lined face. It was obvious that he was of a great age, although his back was unbowed and he moved without any trace of feebleness.

'It is getting late and he has not come,' he said, advancing slowly and standing beside her.

'Perhaps something has happened to delay him,' she answered in a rich contralto with the merest trace of huskiness.

'He said he would be here by midnight, and it is now two hours past,' said the old man. 'I am afraid that something must have happened.'

She turned on her side and put down the jade holder in a tray on a low table by the settee.

'I think he will come,' she said, supporting herself on one elbow and looking up at him. 'I feel sure that he will come.'

'I hope you are right,' he answered. 'It would be terrible if anything should have gone wrong . . . '

'What could go wrong, now?' she demanded.

'There are many things, O my daughter,' said the old man, shaking his head.

'You are tired,' said the girl, getting up with a lithe and graceful movement, and laying a hand affectionately upon his arm. 'It is the result of the strain you have gone through during the last few months. Why don't you rest . . . ?'

The old man shook his head.

'I cannot rest until I know,' he answered. 'So much depends upon the success of his mission.'

'I know,' she said. 'Who should know that better than I? Have I not done as much as anyone?'

'Indeed you have, my daughter,' said the old man. 'But . . . '

'The night is bad,' she went on. 'There is a mist that covers the land like a veil. It is difficult to travel on such a night . . . '

'Khyfami has travelled in worse conditions,' murmured the old man. 'In the sandstorms of the desert, and under the scorching sun. A mist would not delay him . . . '

'Something has delayed him,' said the girl. 'But he will come. Of that I am certain.'

She spoke reassuringly, but deep in the

almond-shaped eyes lurked a hint of anxiety. She was not so sure as she tried to make out. The old man sat down upon a low ebony chair and clasped his wrinkled hands in his lap. His lined face was expressionless and, in the embroidered robe which he wore, he looked more like a grotesque carving in ivory than a living person. His skin was almost transparent, and the blue veins stood out at his temples and in his neck and on the backs of his hands. The girl looked at him with an expression that was a little troubled.

'I wish that you would rest, O my father,' she said.

'I will rest when I have seen Khyfami,' he answered.

'I will call you directly he arrives,' she began persuasively. 'Why don't you . . . '

'I could not rest,' he interrupted.

She sighed, went over to the table by the huge settee, and picked up the jade cigarette holder. From a gold box she took a cigarette and fitted it carefully into the holder. A small, curiously shaped lamp burned beside the box with a pale violet flame, and into this she dipped the end of the cigarette. Blowing out a thin stream of smoke, she crossed the room and pressed a concealed bell push near the fireplace. Almost immediately the door opened and a tall Egyptian, in the robes of a native servant, appeared.

'Bring coffee,' said the girl curtly, and the man bowed and withdrew.

'Karina.' The old man in the chair spoke in almost a whisper.

'Yes?' She came over to his side and bent, down.

'Do you remember that American we met in Cairo?' He could not see her face and was, therefore, unaware of the sudden dusky blush which deepened the tan of her throat and cheeks.

'Yes,' she answered, in a voice that was as low as his own.

'What was his name?' he asked. 'I have been trying to remember . . . '

'Why?' she said, huskily.

'I don't like to forget things,' he answered.

'It was a long time ago.' She was staring over his head into vacancy, as though her mind were bridging the gulf of time. 'Many months . . . '

'But you haven't forgotten, Karina,' he said, gently. 'What was his name?'

'Janson,' she replied. 'Gary Janson . . . '

'Ah, yes, that was it,' said the old man, nodding.

'Why have you suddenly thought of him?' she asked. 'Now . . . ?'

'I don't know,' he said, slowly shaking his head. 'It just came to me . . . I was thinking of Cairo . . . '

2

She was thinking of Cairo, too, now that the old man's question had brought memory flooding back . . . The terrace of Shepherd's Hotel bathed in hot sunshine . . . the magic of the desert in the blue-white light of the moon, with the gleaming Nile like a twisted silver ribbon . . . the Valley of the Kings in the dusky twilight, sombre and glamorised by an ancient enchantment . . . The great Pylon at Karnak, and the Pyramids of Gizeh in the purple haze of the setting sun . . . and Gary Janson with his laughing eyes and quick, one-sided smile that she had found so fascinating and whimsical. Pictures, unfinished and fragmentary, built up and dissolved in rapid succession . . .

'The world is a small place.' The thin voice of the old man broke in on her thoughts and scattered the pictures like the shaking of a kaleidoscope.

'What do you mean?' she asked.

'People meet, and part, and meet again,' he answered, 'if it is so written. I do not think that we have seen the last of the American, Mr. Janson.'

'What makes you think that?' she said. 'He was going back to his own country ... It is many hundreds of miles away ... '

'It is written that we shall see him again,' said the old man, calmly.

She made no reply. The cigarette had burned down to the holder, smouldering away between her fingers, and she pressed out the stub against the side of the ashtray and replaced it with a fresh cigarette from the gold box.

'You are smoking too much, O my daughter,' said the old man. 'It is not good that you should seek to soothe your nerves in that way ... '

'It does not harm me,' she said.

'Everything that is done in excess is harmful,' he retorted. 'The time passes and Khyfami does not come ... '

She had almost forgotten Khyfami in the confusion of mind which the mention of Gary Janson had engendered, although the two were, in a way, connected. Perhaps it would be more accurate to say 'had been,' for Khyfami had been in Cairo, too, during those summer months that seemed so long ago . . .

'He has not come,' repeated the old man, and shook his head sadly. 'I have a feeling that he will not come now.'

The Egyptian servant came in silently before she could reply. He carried a silver tray on which was set a coffee service in dull black china of eggshell thinness. Putting the tray down on a low table beside Karina, he bowed, and as silently withdrew. She poured out the coffee. It was thick and syrupy, and she added a few drops of rose water from a cut-glass container. She put in a spoonful of gum Arabic from a little bowl and carried the cup over to the old man.

'I think you are being very pessimistic,' she said, answering his last remark. 'Khyfami has a long way to come . . . '

'But he is now many hours overdue,' said the old man. He sipped his coffee delicately. 'I cannot but help feeling pessimistic.'

'Many things may have happened to delay him,' said Karina, returning to the table and taking up her own coffee cup. 'I wish you would rest, O my father. You would feel better . . . '

'I feel quite well,' he answered a trifle impatiently. 'Only my mind is disturbed . . . '

The silver tinkle of a bell, soft and muted, but sounding loud in the silence of the house, broke in upon his sentence, and the old man jerked up his head.

'There is Khyfami, now,' exclaimed the girl. 'You see? Your fears were groundless. I said all along that he would come.'

He said nothing, but his eyes turned towards the door and watched it expectantly. After an interval that seemed an age to the two who waited, it opened, and the Egyptian servant ushered in a tall, olive-skinned, dark-eyed man in a heavy overcoat, the fleecy material of which glistened with moisture in the light. He bowed to Karina with a courtliness that held no trace of servility.

'What makes you so late. Khyfami?' asked the old man. 'We have been waiting for you many hours . . . '

'I could not get here any sooner, Harmachis,' said the tall man. 'I fear that now that I am here, I bring bad news . . . '

'You have been unsuccessful?' asked Harmachis, and there was a slight tremor in his thin voice.

'I have been unsuccessful,' answered Khyfami. 'The man is dead . . . '

Karina caught her breath and the old man in the chair uttered a queer little sound that was half a cry and half a groan.

'Dead,' he echoed in a strangled voice. 'Dead . . . '

'Murdered,' said Khyfami. 'Rather horribly . . . '

'How . . . how did it happen?' asked Karina, her face pale.

'I don't know,' answered the tall man. 'Either how it happened, or who did it. I only saw him after . . . '

'The Lamos?' whispered Harmachis hoarsely. 'The Lamps . . . ?'

Khyfami shook his head.

'There is no trace of them,' he said. He

looked from one to the other. 'I had better tell you all that happened,' he said. 'You will understand better so . . . If I might be permitted to sit . . . ?'

'Oh, yes. of course. I am sorry,' said Karina. 'I forgot in the shock . . . '

'It is only natural,' murmured Khyfami. He took off his heavy coat and laid it over the back of a chair.

'You would like some coffee?' said the girl. 'It is fresh . . . '

'Please,' said Khyfami. He sat down in a carved ebony chair. 'It has been a strenuous night,' he went on apologetically. 'I am tired and weary . . . '

She brought him a cup of coffee and offered him a cigarette. He drank the coffee quickly, lighted the cigarette and expelled the smoke from his thin lips slowly. Harmachis said nothing. Immovable, he sat and waited, but he looked older and more shrunken . . .

Khyfami cleared his throat, inhaled the smoke of his cigarette deeply, as though he found it soothing, and began:

'I had an appointment, as you know, early yesterday evening with the man

Karolides at his lodgings in Vauxhall. The final arrangements of our business were to be completed then. Karolides never impressed me as being trustworthy. He was out solely for gain and would be, I knew, prepared to sell what he had to the highest bidder, irrespective of any agreement which he might have come to with us. It was only what he would call 'good business.' When, therefore, I arrived at his lodgings and found that he was out, I was immediately suspicious that things were not going as smoothly as I had hoped. I waited, but the appointed time went by and he did not come. At the expiration of nearly an hour I began to get alarmed. I was convinced that, for some reason or other, Karolides had decided to cancel the business between us. Something had happened to make him change his mind, and I thought, perhaps, there might be something in his lodgings that would suggest what it was. If it should be a better offer, I might still be in time to increase ours.' He paused and drew deeply again at his cigarette. The room was deadly silent. Karina had curled herself up on the golden settee and was listening intently, her almond eyes fixed on his face. The old man in the chair, still motionless as a carven image, stared straight before him, his face utterly devoid of all expression.

'I searched the room,' went on Khyfami, 'and I found a small scrap of paper bearing an address and some figures. It had been hastily scrawled in pencil: 'Berrydale. 18, Hayford Avenue,' and underneath, '5.42.' This might have been the time of an appointment, but it seemed to me more likely that it was the time for the departure of a train. Karolides, I thought, must have gone to this place Berrydale, which I remembered was a short distance down the line, and to 18 Hayford Avenue. It was unlikely that any negotiations he was contemplating would be completed immediately, and, if I could find him, there might still be time to prevent them being completed at all. I decided to go to this address in Berrydale and find out what I could. I hurried to Vauxhall Station and found I had just missed the Berrydale train which stopped there. There was another, I was told, in twenty minutes, and this I caught. It was very foggy when I got out at Berrydale Station, but I enquired my way to Hayford Avenue from the porter and set out.

'I passed a woman on my way, and the reason that I mention this you will see later. I had no difficulty, in spite of the mist, in finding Hayford Avenue. The name was painted clearly on a board at the entrance to the street. Nor was there any difficulty in finding number 18. But when I did find it, I was surprised to discover that it was an empty house. I did not discover this until I had explored the neglected approach and found that the front door was partly open. I could hear nothing within, and I entered. Everything was as black as the middle chamber of the great Pyramid, and as completely and utterly silent. I struck a match and saw that I was standing in a huge, bare hall, thick with dust and cobwebs — and then I saw Karolides. He was lying huddled up in the shadow of a massive staircase, and there was a pool of blood round him . . . I went over and I saw that he was quite dead. His head had been battered almost to pulp. It was a shock, as you can imagine, to find him thus. I was momentarily at a loss to know what to do next, and then I thought that perhaps there was something on him, in his pockets, that would give us the information that we sought. I was just going to search him when I heard footsteps coming up the drive towards the house. I realised that I was in a very unpleasant predicament — if anybody found me there with the murdered body of this man — and I slipped up the staircase and hid myself on the landing.

'I could hear the sounds of somebody out in the porch, and, after an interval, there was a knock that echoed like thunder through the empty house. After another interval the door was pushed open and somebody came in. A little flickering light appeared and then I saw that the person who had come was the woman I had passed earlier. She had ignited a pocket lighter and was standing just inside the hall staring about her.

Presently she saw Karolides. I heard her breath come sharply from her lungs, and then she turned and fled and I heard her footsteps fade away. I waited for a little while and then I ventured down to the hall again and searched the dead man. There was nothing. Somebody had been before me. There was only one sensible thing to do and that was to get away from that house as quickly as I could. If I was found there I should have difficulty in explaining that I had had nothing to do with the murder. Nobody would believe me, particularly the English police, for it could be proved that I had had dealings with Karolides . . . I left, after making sure that there was nobody about, and went back the way I had come. And at the entrance to the street I made an extraordinary discovery. To verify the name of it, I looked again at the board.

It had changed! It was no longer Hayford Avenue, but Court Road . . . '

3

'How could that be?' said Karina, wrinkling her smooth forehead. 'Surely you must have made a mistake?'

Khyfami shook his head.

'There was no mistake,' he answered. 'The name of the road had changed while I had been in that house. How it had done so I will come to presently . . . '

'You found out?' asked the girl.

'Oh, yes, I found out,' he replied. 'I found out a lot of things. You will hear them in their right order . . . '

'The Lamps,' said the old man. 'What of the Lamps, Khyfami?'

'I know nothing of them, Harmachis,' said Khyfami sadly. 'Their whereabouts are unknown, unless it be to the man who killed Karolides . . . '

'Or this woman you spoke of,' said Korina, quickly. 'Who is she and what was she doing at this house where Karolides had been killed?'

'I will continue my story and then you will know all that I know,' said Khyfami. 'Could I, please, have another cup of coffee?'

'It is cold,' said Karina. 'I will ring for some fresh . . . '

'No, no,' interrupted Khyfami. 'Do not trouble. It will do as it is . . . '

She poured him another cup and he drained it thirstily. When she had resumed her place on the settee he went on:

'I was, as I have said, very astonished and surprised to find that the name had altered. I thought at first, as you did, that I must have made a mistake. And then I realised that I could not have done so, for the name had been the same as that which had been written on the piece of paper I had found in Karolides' lodgings, and if it had been Court Road when I had first arrived I should not have entered it. Therefore, it must have changed, or been changed. I examined the board on which it was painted and found that it was firmly fixed to the wall. It had definitely not been moved and replaced so that this must, in reality, be Court Road. If I had seen Hayford Avenue before, it was because a similar sign had been placed *over* the original one. But Karolides had expected to go to 18 Hayford Avenue. That was the address written down. Owing, however, to the change of name, he had actually gone to 18 Court Road, thinking it was the address he sought. The person who had murdered him had tricked him into an empty house. But that meant that there was actually a number eighteen Hayford Avenue, the house to which he had intended going, and it must be somewhere near. You will understand that all this passed through my mind very quickly — far more quickly than it takes me to put it into words. If I could find this house — the real 18 Hayford Avenue — it might help me in my object, which was to once more get on the track of the Lamps. I cast around in the mist and presently I found it. Hayford Avenue was the next road to Court Road, and number eighteen was a large house that was decidedly not empty. I did not wish to make my presence known to the inmates.

I had no idea who lived there, and it might not be strategic. I was, however, determined to find out who occupied it. I was lurking about, trying to decide how I could achieve this purpose, when a car drew up a little way away and the woman who had run from the empty house got out — I recognised her from the coat she wore — and with her was a very fat man and a police constable.

'They entered the gate of number eighteen and, later, were admitted to the house. After a while they came out again, and I followed them when they walked up Hayford Avenue and into Court Road. They all three went into the empty house, but presently the woman and the police constable came out again, leaving the fat man behind. It was evident that she had told the police about her discovery, but I couldn't understand why they had not come straight to the empty house. What did she know about the other house? I hung about for most of the evening; saw Karolides' body taken away, and the counterfeit boards which had been used to change the road names found in some bushes of a house further up the street. When it began to grow late I concluded that there was nothing more I could do there and it was dangerous, with the police in the vicinity, to remain. If I was seen lurking about they might arrest me on suspicion. I made my way back to the railway station and, passing a telephone box, suddenly saw how I could find out the name of the occupant of 18 Hayford Avenue. I rang up the exchange and asked them if they could give me the telephone number for that address. They did so, and I put through a call. A woman's voice answered. She said: 'This is Professor Locksley's house' . . . That was all I wished to know, so I just said 'Wrong number' and hung up the receiver . . . '

'Professor Locksley, the great authority on Ancient Egypt?' broke in the old man.

'Yes,' said Khyfami. 'Very significant, don't you think?'

'Do you mean that Karolides was going to negotiate with him about the Lamps?' exclaimed the girl.

Khyfami nodded.

'Yes,' he answered. 'I think it is obvious that was his intention . . . '

'And somebody lured him by a trick to the empty house instead and killed him,' said Karina, frowning. 'Who could it be?'

Khyfami spread his hands in a gesture that signified his complete lack of ideas on the subject.

'Who can tell?' he said. 'Somebody who knew about the arrangement Karolides had made behind our backs, obviously. Somebody who now holds the secret of the Lamps . . . '

'He must be found,' said Harmachis. 'He must be found and forced to disclose his secret. The Lamps must be recovered and restored . . . '

Slowly Khyfami nodded. Into his strong, clear-cut face came a look of hesitancy and indecision. Karina saw it and, wondering at its cause, said: 'What is it, Khyfami? You have something on your mind . . . '

'Yes,' answered Khyfami. He hesitated, and then went on: 'There is something that I had not told you. I had almost decided that I would *not* tell you . . . '

'Why?' she demanded.

'Because I did not want to cause you trouble and pain,' he said. 'But I think you should, perhaps, know. It may be better if you know . . . '

'I don't understand . . . ' she began, and he interrupted her abruptly.

'While I was waiting and watching the empty house in Court Road,' he said, 'while the police were conducting their investigations, a man walked down the street. I was concealed in the garden of a house and he could not see me, but I could see him — I could see him clearly, because he passed under a lamp and it shone full upon him . . . '

'Do you mean you recognised him?' she asked.

'Yes, I recognised him,' said Khyfami. 'It was the young American we met in Cairo . . . '

'Gary Janson?' she whispered.

'Yes,' he replied, nodding. 'That was the man — Gary Janson.'

4

Karina stared at him, her almond-shaped eyes wide and her lips parted.

'You are *sure*?' she whispered, after a pause.

'Oh, yes, I am quite sure,' said Khyfami.

'But he was going back to America,' she said.

'There has been time for him to do that, and to come back here,' said Khyfami.

'But . . . but he couldn't be mixed up in this,' she said. 'What could it have to do with him?'

'I said that it was written we should meet him again,' said Harmachis, tonelessly.

'Yes . . . yes, you did.' She looked at him in astonished bewilderment. 'How could you know? How *did* you know . . . ?'

'It was written,' said the old man. 'Things do not happen by chance and without reason, though sometimes it may seem so. The young American in Cairo did not meet us only to pass out of our lives. There was a purpose in that contact which was not fulfilled — then. Therefore, he was bound to cross our path again in order that that purpose should *be* fulfilled.'

'You may be right,' she said. 'You are wiser than I, O my father. But what could he have been doing in this place — what is it?'

'Berrydale,' said Khyfami. 'I know not what he could have been doing there. But his presence was not a coincidence. Of that I am sure . . . '

'There is no such thing as a coincidence,' said Harmachis. 'What is called a coincidence by those ignorant of the Law is the working of the Plan . . . '

'I used the word unthinkingly,' said Khyfami, apologetically. 'You are right, Harmachis, of course.'

'How could Gary Janson know anything about Karolides?' demanded Karina, in perplexity.

'That is something we shall have to find out,' said the old man, rising to his feet and beginning to pace up and down the room. 'We must also discover who this woman is and what brought her to that house where Karolides was murdered. There is much to be done, and done quickly. This unknown person who possesses the secret of the Lamps must be found, before he can dispose of his knowledge . . . '

'If he has it,' put in Khyfami. 'We have no proof that the secret was in Karolides' possession when he was killed. We know he had it, but did he take it with him?'

'That is true,' agreed Harmachis.

'He was going to see Professor Locksley, and we believe that it was in connection with the Lamps, but we are not *sure*,' went on Khyfami. 'Karolides dabbled in many strange things. He was what is called a crook, and he was playing some game for his own ends. Perhaps he would take the precaution of not carrying the secret of the Lamps about with him.'

'You mean that his murderer may have searched him in vain?' said the old man. 'Yes, that is a possibility. You knew this man, Karolides. I did not. You would know how he would be likely to act . . . '

'He was of a very secretive nature,' said Khyfami. 'The sort of man of whom they say here that 'he does not like to let his right hand know what his left hand is doing.' He was also very distrustful of people . . . '

'The type of man who judges others by himself,' murmured Harmachis, nodding. 'Yes, I can well believe that such a man would carry nothing of value on his person.'

'There is always the possibility,' remarked Khyfami, 'that he did not consign the secret of the Lamps to writing. He may have kept it in his mind.'

'If that is so then it is lost for ever,' said Harmachis, with a note of despair in his thin voice.

'Unless he told whoever killed him before he died,' said Khyfami. 'If he was murdered because of the secret, the murderer would hardly have been so foolish as to destroy him before he had learned it . . . '

'But who is this murderer?' cried the old man. 'He is as unknown to us as the whereabouts of the Lamps . . . '

'That must be rectified,' said Khyfami quietly. 'He must be found . . . '

'One grain of sand in a desert,' answered Harmachis, shaking his white head. 'A drop of water in the Red Sea, a single tree in a forest. How do you propose to seek him?'

'Perhaps this man, Professor Locksley, could help,' said Khyfami. 'The murderer must have had pre-knowledge that Karolides was going to see this Professor, otherwise he could not have worked his trick of changing the road names . . . '

'Great discretion would have to be exercised,' said the old man. 'Professor Locksley would try to acquire the Lamps for himself . . . '

'I will go,' said Karina. 'I will find an excuse to see this Professor Locksley and find out what I can . . . '

'You will have to be careful . . . ' began Khyfami.

'I will be,' said the girl, and Harmachis nodded approvingly.

'It will be best for you to do this, O my daughter,' he said. 'But your excuse must be a good one. You must not let them think that you have any connection with Karolides. That would be dangerous . . . '

'I will find a good excuse,' said Karina.

'And there is the woman,' went on Harmachis. 'The woman who brought the police . . . '

'You can leave her to me,' said Khyfami, quietly.

5

Jill Hartley woke after a restless and disturbed night and, in the intermediate state before the full possession of her senses returned to her, wondered what could have happened to change her room during the night ... and then she remembered and sat up, pushing the hair back from her forehead. This, of course, was Professor Locksley's house. He had insisted upon her staying after the exciting events of the previous evening. The plain, rather old-fashioned nightgown she was wearing belonged to Mrs. Moule, the housekeeper ...

There was a tap at the door and Mrs. Moule herself came in with a small tray of tea.

'Good-morning, Miss,' she said. 'I hope you slept comfortably?'

Jill hadn't. She had been awake for the greater part of the night and had not fallen into a real sleep until the early hours, but she didn't like to say so.

'Yes, thank you,' she answered. 'What time is it?'

'A quarter to eight, Miss,' said the housekeeper, putting down the tray on a small table by the bedside. 'Breakfast will be ready at half-past.'

She withdrew, and Jill poured herself out a cup of tea and sipped it gratefully. She had a slight headache, which she decided was the result of her disturbed night. She wondered if anything further had happened after she had gone to bed. She had heard Professor Locksley moving about for quite a long time, and once she wakened from a partial doze and thought she heard the murmur of voices . . . There would be quite a lot to tell Mr. Tape when she got back. She pictured his astonished face and smiled . . .

After her second cup of tea her headache went, and she got up. The sight of herself in the old-fashioned frilled nightgown, reflected in the cheval mirror, made her laugh. She looked so very prim and proper; the product of a bygone age. The contrast between it and her own dainty, flimsy nightwear was startling. Mrs. Moule had provided a dressing-gown of sorts and, putting this on, she went in search of the bathroom. She heard a clock somewhere below strike the half-hour as she finished dressing, and went downstairs. A smell of coffee led her to the dining room, where she found Richard Wayland reading the morning paper.

'Hello,' he greeted, laying the paper down as she came in. 'You're bright and early this morning . . .'

'I am bright and early every morning,' she retorted. 'I have to be at work at nine o'clock, usually.'

'What a dreadful thought,' he said, grinning at her. 'I don't usually appear at this ungodly hour. I made an exception this morning out of deference to you . . .'

'You needn't have bothered,' she said, coolly. 'I much prefer to breakfast alone.'

'So does any sensible person,' he replied. 'A most unsociable meal, break-fast. Now, dinner is another matter . . . Where shall we dine this evening?'

'You can dine where you like,' she said,

sitting down and pouring out a cup of coffee. '*I* am dining at my own flat . . . '

'Still adamant?' He made a grimace. 'All right. We'll bring the subject up again later.'

'You can save yourself a great deal of trouble if you forget all about it, Mr. Wayland,' she said. 'I have no intention of dining with you tonight, or any other night.'

'Try the bacon and eggs,' he suggested, quite unabashed, as she looked at the dishes on the sideboard. 'I'll help you to some.' He got up, took a plate, and began to serve out eggs and bacon. 'You know,' he went on, as he brought the laden plate back and set it before her, 'for such a soft and lovely exterior you have a hard internal core that makes granite look like putty.'

'Thank you, Mr. Wayland,' she said.

'You must miss a lot of fun,' he said, shaking his head sadly.

'That depends a great deal on one's idea of fun,' she answered, helping herself to toast.

'It's incredible,' he murmured, looking

at her thoughtfully.

'Were you never told, Mr. Wayland,' she said, calmly going on with her breakfast, 'that it is the height of rudeness to stare?'

'A thing of beauty is a joy for ever,' he answered, and to her annoyance she found herself reddening. 'What time do you finish work at Tape's office?'

'I really cannot see what concern that is of yours,' she replied.

'You can't?' he remarked, raising his eyebrows. 'I don't think that is quite a truthful statement, is it? However, we'll let it go. I shall be waiting outside for you at six o'clock.'

Before she could reply to this with a suitably vitriolic retort, the door opened and Professor Locksley came in.

'Good morning, Miss — er — Hartley,' he said. 'I trust you slept well? Good morning, Richard. It is rather unusual to see you before lunch . . . '

'I thought Jill could probably do with a bit of cheering up,' replied Richard, 'so I overcame my usual morning sloth and rose with the proverbial lark.'

Professor Locksley looked from one to

the other with the suspicion of a twinkle in his eyes.

'I hope, Miss Hartley,' he said, 'that my graceless nephew has been behaving himself?'

'His behaviour has been characteristic,' said Jill.

'I feared as much,' said Locksley. He went over to the sideboard and peered short-sightedly at the dishes.

'I recommend the eggs and bacon,' said Richard. 'Jill is having dinner with me this evening . . . '

'I'm doing nothing of the sort!' she declared, indignantly.

'Oh, come now,' protested Richard, wickedly. 'You promised. You can't go back on a promise. Don't be shy in front of Uncle.'

'I . . . I . . . ' For a moment she was speechless.

'What did you want to butt in for just then?' said Richard. 'Jill and I were getting along nicely . . . '

'Mr. Wayland!' She looked at him with a flushed face and angry eyes. 'We were *not* getting along nicely and I *never* promised that I would have dinner with you. I told you I had no intention whatever of doing so . . . '

'Six o'clock, outside Tape's office,' he murmured, winking at her. 'That was the arrangement . . . '

'It was *your* arrangement,' she broke in furiously. 'I never agreed to anything of the kind . . . '

'Don't let my nephew annoy you, Miss Hartley,' said Professor Locksley mildly, coming back to the table with a heaped plate. 'He has a queer and pawky sense of humour . . . '

'I never made any arrangement to meet him,' said Jill.

'I'm quite sure you didn't,' said Locksley, sitting down. 'I have not the slightest doubt that he did all the arranging. Unfortunately he has never learned the meaning of the word 'No' when it applies to anything that he wishes to do . . . '

'Well, this will be a new experience for him,' said Jill, shortly. She was thoroughly annoyed and she showed it; to Richard Wayland's huge delight.

'I like new experiences,' he declared, lighting a cigarette and blowing the smoke towards the ceiling. 'Life would be dull and drab without new experiences . . . '

'Why not try speaking the truth?' she suggested unkindly, but he only grinned at her amiably.

'We'll go further into the matter this evening,' he said.

'Now, now,' interposed Professor Locksley, much as he might have addressed a small boy. 'That'll do, Richard. I can't allow you to annoy Miss Hartley in this way. She has had a very unpleasant experience, and I don't expect that she feels in the mood for your ridiculous nonsense . . . '

'I'm sorry,' said Richard, quickly. 'I'm a stupid idiot. I forgot . . . '

'I haven't,' remarked Locksley, a little grimly. 'I have to go to the mortuary this morning to see if I can identify this man. It's an abominable nuisance.'

Jill's face puckered distastefully.

'I'm glad they didn't ask me,' she said. 'I don't think I shall ever forget the sight of that huge, shadowy hall . . . Ugh! It was horrid . . . '

'I don't suppose they'll bother you much,' said Professor Locksley. 'You'll have to attend the inquest, of course, but after that I don't suppose they'll worry you. You've told them all you know . . . '

'There's something I can't remember,' said Jill, frowning. 'Something about that horrible house . . . '

'What do you mean?' asked Richard, quickly, and she shook her head.

'I don't know,' she confessed, with a puzzled look. 'It's something that I feel I ought to remember, and yet I can't think what it is . . . '

'What sort of thing?' he inquired. Again she shook her head.

'It was something I *saw*,' she answered. 'It's all very confused, and I didn't remember it at all until just after I went to bed . . . It was only an impression even then . . . '

'What kind of an impression?' said Professor Locksley.

'It's rather difficult to describe,' she said, slowly. 'There was something *missing* the second time I looked at that hall . . . when I went back with the police . . . '

'Something missing?' echoed Richard.

She nodded.

'Yes. At least, that's the impression I got. There was something there when I *first* saw the hall which *wasn't* there when I saw it again. I didn't think of it at the time. It was only after . . . '

'And you've no idea what it was?' said Wayland.

'No. It's all very vague, but I have a queer feeling that I *ought* to remember,' she replied. 'That it's something *important . . .* '

'It will probably come back to you, Miss Hartley,' said Locksley, 'if you don't try and force it. I have frequently experienced the same thing — a peculiar hiatus in the memory . . . '

'What makes you imagine that it should be important. Jill?' asked Richard, curiously.

'I don't know,' she answered. 'I just feel that it is . . . '

'Don't you think that you may have imagined it . . . ?'

'No, I'm sure there was *something* . . . It was there the first time and it wasn't the second . . . '

'You realise what that would mean, if you are right?' remarked Richard, seriously. 'It would mean that somebody was either in that house while you were there, or came back between the time you left and returned with the police . . . '

'Yes, I suppose so,' she interpolated.

' . . . And that it was probably the murderer,' he ended gravely.

6

The Assistant Commissioner looked across his desk at the obese figure of Mr. Budd. and fiddled with a pencil.

'It seems to be a very queer business,' he remarked, thoughtfully. 'Very queer indeed . . . '

'Yes, sir,' murmured the stout superintendent, suppressing a yawn.

'You say you haven't succeeded yet in identifying the dead man?' went on Colonel Blair.

'No, sir,' answered Mr. Budd. 'Professor Locksley 'ad a look at him, but affirms that he is a complete stranger. We're checking up on his fingerprints. They may lead to sump'n . . . '

'What about the girl?' asked the Assistant Commissioner. 'This Jill Hartley. Anything known about her?'

'Only to her credit, sir,' replied the big man, shifting in his chair and drawing forth a protesting creak from that ill-used piece of furniture. 'I've bin in touch with Mr. Tape, her employer, and he vouches for her good character. I don't think she knows anything about it, sir, other than she's said . . . '

'Well, it's a queer business altogether,' said Colonel Blair, with a certain lack of originality in his phrasing. 'This mention of Seven Lamps . . . what do you make of that?'

Mr. Budd shrugged hs massive shoulders slightly.

'I don't make nothin' of it — yet, sir,' he said. 'Professor Locksley read out a lot o' rigmarole from an old book about Seven Lamps that was 'idden somewhere in a pyramid, but it was written five thousand years ago . . . '

'Don't despise it on that account,' interrupted the Assistant Commissioner. 'If these lamps have been found they would probably be very valuable to a great many people.'

'I'm not despisin' it, sir,' said Mr. Budd. 'As a motive for killin' this feller, it 'ud probably be a pretty good one, but there's no proof that these lamps *was* found. That scrap o' paper only mentions 'em . . . '

'But that seems to suggest that they are definitely connected with the murder,' said Colonel Blair.

'Maybe,' admitted the big man, cautiously. 'I'm not overlookin' that, sir. The first thin' we've got to do is to identify the dead man. We'll probably know a lot more about it, then. Once we know who 'e was, we can find out all about 'im. Maybe these lamps 'ull crop up again then . . . '

'I should say it was very likely,' remarked the Assistant Commissioner, passing a hand over the top of his neat, grey head and gently smoothing the immaculate hair. 'In my opinion this man was either in possession of these lamps, or knew where they were to be found. He realised their immense value and was on his way to Professor Locksley when he was tricked into this empty house and murdered . . . That seems to be a reasonable theory on the facts as we know them at present.'

'Yes, sir,' agreed Mr. Budd. 'That

would seem ter be somethin' like it . . . '

'You'll take charge of the inquiry, of course,' said Colonel Blair. 'You're not on anything important just now. You'd better take Sergeant Leek to help you . . . '

'Yes, sir,' murmured Mr. Budd, getting ponderously to his feet.

'Keep me informed of your progress,' said the Assistant Commissioner. 'This is an unusual affair, and I am particularly interested . . . '

Mr. Budd left the office and with portly dignity made his way slowly to his own small, cheerless room. Sergeant Leek was dozing uncomfortably on a hard chair against the wall, but he blinked into wakefulness as his superior came in.

'Don't you get enough sleep at home?' demanded Mr. Budd, irritably, as he squeezed himself into his desk chair and took a cigar from his waistcoat pocket.

'I wasn't asleep.' Leek surveyed him with his usual injured expression. 'I was just ponderin' . . . '

'On your misspent life, I've no doubt,' snarled Mr. Budd, biting off the end of the cigar and searching for his matches.

'Well, you won't 'ave any time for ponderin' from now on. We've bin assigned to the Berrydale murder, an' you're goin' to be kept busy.'

The sergeant's long, melancholy face did not light up with joy at the news. If anything, he looked a little more gloomy and depressed.

'That's that empty 'ouse business you was tellin' me about, ain't it?' he said.

Mr. Budd nodded, struck a match and lit his cigar.

'That's it,' he said. 'So you can confine all yer sleepin' to your bedroom — an' I don't s'pose yer'll see much of that,' he added with great satisfaction, blowing out a poisonous cloud of rank, evil-smelling smoke.

Sergeant Leek coughed as it drifted under his thin nose.

'From what you told me,' he remarked mournfully, 'it looks like bein' a difficult job.'

'It looks like being a *very* difficult job,' agreed the big man, leaning back in his chair and sleepily gazing at the ceiling. 'Do you know anythin' about Egypt?'

'Egypt?' said the astonished Leek. 'That's where the Sphinx is, ain't it?'

'And other things,' murmured Mr. Budd. 'Peculiar thin's from all accounts ... 'All the mystery and glamour o' the East,' as the advertisements say ... 'Ave you ever 'eard of Anubis, Osiris, Isis an' Thoth?'

Leek shook his head in bewilderment.

'Can't say I 'ave,' he replied. 'Who are they? Crooks . . . ?'

'They was gods,' said Mr. Budd. severely. 'Ancient Egyptian gods, an' there was a whole lot more of 'em that I can't remember. The gods of Ancient Egypt were very prolific. There must 'ave bin nearly as many gods as people from what I can make out ... '

The melancholy sergeant looked a little bored.

'What's it got ter do with us?' he asked, practically.

'It may have a lot,' said Mr. Budd, and at that moment there was a tap at the door and a messenger entered.

'From the Record Department, sir,' he said, laying down a folder on the desk.

'An' will you return it at once when you've finished with it, sir?'

'I will,' said Mr. Budd, hoisting himself forward and opening the folder with interest. 'Looks as though we're goin' ter be lucky,' he remarked, when the messenger had gone.

'What's that, then?' asked the sergeant, getting up and drifting over to his side.

'This,' replied Mr. Budd, 'is the record of the dead man — don't breathe down my neck, it tickles — I sent 'is fingerprints to be checked up on the off chance that 'e had a police record, an' it seems 'e 'ad. H'm,' he commented, as he read the sheets before him, 'he certainly 'ad! He was a Greek an' his name was Arturus Karolides . . . four convictions altogether . . . H'm . . . Specialised in paintings an' antiques . . . H'm . . . believed to be a receiver of stolen property on a large scale . . . Well, well . . . believed to have been responsible for smuggling stolen masterpieces to the United States for sale to collectors . . . So this is the feller, it it? . . . Last known address 14 Cumberland Street, Vauxhall . . . Well, there we are.

The feller who was murdered in the empty 'ouse in Court Road, Berrydale, was Arturus Karolides, a Greek crook.' He shut the folder and leaned back, chewing at the end of his cigar. 'Interestin' an' peculiar. All we've got ter do now is to find out who killed 'im an' why. Get your hat.'

'Where are we goin'?' asked Leek.

'To 14 Cumberland Street, Vauxhall,' answered Mr. Budd, promptly. 'There's quite a lot about Mr. Karolides in this record, but I want ter know more . . . '

7

Cumberland Street was not a very salubrious neighbourhood. The houses were grimy and drab, like most of the houses in that district, and children were playing noisily in the roadway. No. 14 was a little cleaner than the others, but not much, and when Mr. Budd knocked there was a long delay before anyone answered, and then the door was opened by a tired-looking woman with wisps of grey hair straggling over her lined face, and her bare arms wet with soap-suds.

'Mr. Karolides live 'ere?' asked the big man.

''E ain't in,' snapped the woman, shortly, and started to shut the door.

'Just a minute, Ma'am,' said Mr. Budd. 'Are you the landlady?'

'We're full up,' said the woman.

'We're not looking for rooms,' said the stout superintendent. 'I'm a police officer from Scotland Yard, and I'd like to have a word with you . . . '

The woman's face changed. Apprehension, fear, curiosity, and that peculiar truculence with which her type greet any representative of authority, passed in rapid succession over her wan face.

'Wot's 'e done?' she demanded.

'Who?' asked Mr. Budd.

'Karolides,' she said.

'I think we could talk better inside,' he suggested, gently.

She hesitated. It was evidently against her principles to invite the police into her establishment.

'Awl right, come in,' she said at last, ungraciously. 'But I'm very busy. I'm doin' some washin' an' . . . '

'I won't keep yer longer'n I can help,' said Mr. Budd, stepping into the dingy hall. 'It's rather a serious matter . . . '

'What's 'e been up to?' said the woman, closing the door and facing them, her hands fumbling with her grimy apron.

'It's a matter o' murder, I'm afraid . . . ' began Mr. Budd, and she uttered an exclamation.

'Cripes!' she cried. 'Who's 'e done in . . . ?'

'It was Karolides who was murdered,' said Mr. Budd. 'I should like to see his rooms, and ask you a few questions . . . '

'I don't know nothing about 'im,' she declared, hastily. 'I can't tell you nuthin', mister . . . '

'What's your name, Ma'am?' interrupted the big man.

'Regan — Alice Regan,' she answered sullenly. 'I don't know anything about this . . . I've never been in no trouble before . . . '

'You aren't in any trouble now, Ma'am,' said Mr. Budd cheerfully. 'All you've got ter do is answer a few questions. Is it Mrs. Regan?'

She nodded.

'Husband livin' 'ere?'

''E's bin dead over three years . . . '

'Well, now, Mrs. Regan,' said Mr. Budd, 'this man Karolides has been stayin' with you for how long?'

'Two months short o' three years,' she answered. 'But 'e didn't stay 'ere all the time. Sometimes 'e was away for several weeks at a stretch. 'E kep' 'is rooms on, though, an' always paid regular . . . '

'Did he have many visitors?'

'Not many.'

'Did he say where 'e was goin' when he went out yesterday?'

'No, 'e never said where 'e was goin' when 'e went out. Why should 'e? It wasn't none o' my business . . . '

'I thought 'e might have mentioned it. Can you remember the names of any of the people who came to see 'im?'

'I never 'eard their names. There was a foreigner what come several times an' a little feller who called once or twice. Somethin' like a music 'all comic ter look at, 'e was. The foreign feller was 'ere last evenin' . . . '

'Oh, he was, eh?' said Mr. Budd, with interest.

'Mr. Karolides 'ad already gone out, but 'e said 'e 'ad an appointment with 'im, an' so I let him go up an' wait.'

'What was this man like?' asked the superintendent. But Mrs. Regan was vague. He was tall and dark and very well-dressed. That was the best she could do in the way of description. He had been to see Karolides half-a-dozen times perhaps. They seemed quite friendly. She had never heard of Professor Locksley, but then, she'd already said she didn't know anything, hadn't she?

Mr. Budd exhausted his questions and asked to see the rooms occupied by Karolides. She took them upstairs to the first floor. Her late lodger had rented the front room and the one next to it as sitting room and bedroom respectively. The sitting room was a fair-sized apartment overlooking the dingy street. The furniture was shabby and cheap, but the place was clean, and Karolides had added one or two articles of his own that made the room look fairly comfortable.

'If yer don't want me for a bit I'll go an' get on with me washing,' said Mrs. Regan, 'afore the water gets stone cold . . . '

Receiving permission to depart, she shuffled hurriedly away, and they heard her loose shoes flapping as she descended the stairs.

'I wonder who this dark, foreign-lookin' feller was?' remarked Mr. Budd, looking sleepily about him. 'Sounds as if it might be important. We'll 'ave ter try and locate 'im. Meanwhile, let's see what we can find 'ere.'

With Leek's assistance he began a methodical search of the room. The late Mr. Karolides had, apparently, been an extremely careful man, for there was nothing at all that showed on what business he had been engaged, or anything about him. There were no letters or documents of any kind. They tried the bedroom, next door, with no better result. There was a wardrobe with several well-cut suits in it, but there was nothing in any of the pockets. Mr. Budd went back to the sitting room in profound disappointment and stared reflectively, rubbing the lowest of his many chins.

'Looks a bit of a wash-out, don't it?' he murmured. 'Anybody'd think 'e knew he was goin' ter get killed an' 'ad taken the precaution to destroy everythin' concernin' himself before 'e left. Or maybe he was just naturally cautious . . .'

119

'There's somethin' 'ere,' said Leek suddenly. He had gone over to the fireplace and, stooping, peered up the chimney. 'Only a scrap o' paper — blew up with the draught . . . '

He picked it off the side of the chimney delicately, and brought it over to his superior. It was only a small charred scrap, part of a burned letter, apparently, for there was some writing on one side. Mr. Budd took it nearer the window and managed to decipher the scrawl ' . . . *'tonight . . . 9.30 . . . Sacred Ibis . . . L. Glomm,'* stands for Lew Glomm, unless I'm a Hottentot . . . '

'That's the feller who got a stretch fer pinchin' Lady What-d'yer-callem's jewels, ain't it?' broke in Leek.

'That's the feller,' said Mr. Budd. ''E was released about eighteen months ago an' 'as been lyin' pretty low ever since. It looks as if Karolides 'ad an appointment with 'im at some time. There's no tellin' when this was written, though I shouldn't think it had been up that chimney very long by the look of it. What made you look?'

120

'You know me . . . ' began Leek, with great self-complacency.

'That's why I'm surprised,' grunted Mr. Budd. 'The Sacred Ibis. H'm . . . '

'What's that mean?' asked the lean sergeant.

'The Sacred Ibis is a pretty unsavoury club near Limehouse, run by a feller called Ahmadun, an Egyptian . . . '

'An Egyptian?' repeated Leek, and Mr. Budd nodded.

'Yes,' he said. 'There's a lot of Egypt in this business, ain't there? Some pretty queer things 'ave 'appened at The Sacred Ibis, 'an it used to keep 'K' Division fairly busy at one time . . . ' He put the charred scrap of paper carefully away in his pocketbook. 'I think we might pay a visit to The Sacred Ibis an' see if we can find Lew Glomm,' he went on, ruminatively. 'Maybe there's still some queer things goin' on there . . . '

PART THREE

THE SACRED IBIS

1

Jill Hartley put the cover on her type-writer with a sigh of relief. It was a quarter past six and she felt very tired, in spite of the fact that she had not reached the office until two o'clock that afternoon. Mr. Tape had been very sympathetic, but it had not prevented him from asking innumerable questions concerning her adventure of the previous evening. He had, apparently, heard the bare details from the police, and this had only whetted his appetite for more. She told him all she knew, which wasn't much, and he listened with great intentness and interest.

'A — um — most unpleasant experience,' he commented. 'Most unpleasant and — er — upsetting. Dear me, some really terrible things happen in the world, don't they? We read about them constantly in our newspapers, but we never realise how really dreadful they are until we are actually brought into personal contact with them. I am extremely sorry that you should have had to suffer such an experience, particularly as I was, in a way, partly responsible. Um — ah — did you bring back the receipt from Professor Locksley? Ah, yes, thank you, Miss Hartley . . . '

He had given her a long and intricate lease to type, which required a great deal of care and concentration, and kept her occupied for the remainder of the afternoon. There was still nearly a third of it to do when she saw the time and prepared to go home. She attributed her tiredness to her restless night. She would, she thought, have a light meal when she got home, and go straight to bed. The illusive memory which had bothered her was still niggling at her mind. What *was* it that she had seen in that bare and dusty hall? *What* had been missing on that second occasion? She tried to picture the place in her mind's eye, but it was no good. That vague and uncertain memory refused to function.

She tidied her desk, washed her hands,

and put on her hat and coat. She was the last to leave; Mr. Tape had gone early and the junior clerk was always away on the first stroke of six. Thank goodness, she thought, as she came down the gloomy stairs, there was no fog tonight. It was clear and cold; a fairly heavy frost from the look of it; her breath came in white clouds as she pushed open the swing door and emerged into the street . . .

'You're late!' said a voice, cheerfully, and a man's figure loomed out of the gloom.

'Mr. Wayland!' she exclaimed in annoyance.

'Don't look so surprised,' he said, grinning at her. 'I said I'd be here, didn't I . . . ?'

She stopped and faced him, her eyes shining with anger.

'Mr. Wayland,' she said. 'I told you this morning that I had no intention of meeting you tonight . . . '

'You haven't met me,' he retorted, before she could finish. 'I've met *you*! There's a very comfortable little restaurant, a few minutes' walk from here, where the food is excellent . . . '

'I hope you will enjoy it,' she snapped furiously. 'Good night!' She turned abruptly and walked rapidly away. It was insufferable that he should force himself on her like this . . . intolerable . . . He caught up with her and fell into step at her side.

'Look here, Jill,' he said. 'Don't be cross . . . '

'I *am* cross,' she answered. 'I'm very tired, and I want to go home . . . '

'Well, let me walk as far as that with you,' he urged.

'I'd much rather you didn't,' she said.

'You don't like me, do you?' he remarked.

'I don't like your methods,' she retorted. 'I object to people who try and ride roughshod over other people's inclinations.' It was rather a stilted speech and she realised it, which did not improve her temper.

'I'm sorry,' he said, 'because I like *you* very much. I find something very refreshing about you, Jill . . . '

'It sounds as though you were referring

to a new cocktail,' she said. He laughed.

'It wasn't intended like that,' he said. 'Why can't we be friends ... '

'There's no reason why we should be,' she answered. 'In any case, you're not going the best way about it, are you?'

'I did it more for a joke than anything else,' he said. 'I thought it would amuse you ... '

'I don't find it at all amusing,' she said, curtly. 'I should be much more amused if you would leave me alone.'

He sighed.

'You're a difficult girl to please,' he remarked, ruefully.

She did not answer, and for a time they walked along in silence.

'Have you remembered what you were trying to remember at breakfast?' he asked, presently. She shook her head.

'No,' she answered.

'I wonder what it was you thought you saw?' he said.

'I don't know. I've been trying to remember, but I can't.' She stopped before a block of flats. 'This is where I live, Mr. Wayland, so I'll say goodnight ... '

'You're quite certain you wouldn't like some dinner?' he said, hopefully. 'You could go home directly afterwards . . . '

'I'm quite certain, thank you,' she answered. 'Goodnight, Mr. Wayland.'

'Goodnight, Jill,' he said. 'I'll give you a ring and ask you again.'

'You'll only be wasting your time,' she said, and left him

Her flat was on the second floor, and she opened the front door with a sense of relief. Going through into the tiny kitchen she put on the kettle to boil and then took off her hat and coat. She had a slight headache for which she, rather unreasonably, blamed Richard Wayland. If his persistence had not made her in such a temper, she probably wouldn't have got it. She hadn't had one when she had left the office. She boiled herself some eggs, cut some bread and butter, and made a pot of tea. Setting her meal on a tray, she carried it into her comfortable little sitting room, switched on the electric fire, lit the lamp, drew the curtains, and settled down cosily in an armchair to enjoy her frugal dinner in peace and comfort.

It was nice to be alone, she thought, as she ate. Nice to be able to relax completely. She was glad she had succeeded in getting rid of Richard Wayland. Perhaps, after the snubbing she had given him, he would leave her alone in future. She had a feeling that he wouldn't, but she hoped that he would. He must be very thick-skinned or abnormally conceited. Probably a little bit of both. No doubt he had found these methods successful before. Maybe he thought that she didn't mean what she said. Well, he would quickly find out that she did. If he *should* ring up, she would make it quite clear, once and for all, that she had no intention of allowing him to pester her . . .

She finished her meal, smoked a cigarette, and then washed up the dirty things and turned on a bath. For half an hour she lay revelling in boiling hot water, scented with a handful of bath salts, and felt all the weariness seep out of her body. Clad warmly and comfortably in a dressing gown, she did several odd jobs about the flat and, at nine o'clock, was in bed with a book. The niggling memory still haunted her, but she tried resolutely to forget it, though not altogether with complete success. The picture of that gloomy hall kept on rising up before her, blotting out the printed page of her book. If only she could remember *what* it was she had seen . . .

It was raining outside, she could hear the patter of it on the window, and as she became drowsy she turned off the light and snuggled down into her pillow . . . In a few seconds she was asleep . . .

2

Something woke her with a start. One moment she was asleep and the next she was wide awake, staring into the darkness of the room, her heart thumping loudly. She had not been dreaming. This sudden wakefulness was not the result of a nightmare . . . it was something more tangible, but what? She lay still, listening. But there was no sound. The flat was silent. Outside, the rain was still falling heavily. Perhaps it was the sound of that which had awakened her. Her eyes were growing accustomed to the gloom, and she was able to distinguish the shadowy outlines of the familiar furniture. The room was not quite dark. There was a street lamp outside, and its light penetrated the thin curtains and filled the bedroom with a faint glow. And quite suddenly she *did* hear something. It was a scarcely audible sound, and it came from somewhere in the flat — a very gentle creak . . . The kitchen door! One of the hinges always creaked like that when it was opened . . .

Jill felt herself grow cold and rigid. There was somebody in the flat. They had come by the fire escape which ran up close by the kitchen window . . . She listened, straining her ears, stiff with a sudden fear . . . But now she could hear nothing. Perhaps she had been mistaken. Perhaps the door had moved slightly in a draught . . . Only there should be no draught . . . There was a faint click and a soft movement . . . She had not been mistaken. There *was* somebody in the flat! She felt her mouth and throat go suddenly dry as a flood of terror overwhelmed her. Who was it, and what did they want? Was it a burglar . . . ?

She heard the shuffle of a step on the carpet outside the door — a stealthy sound as though someone were *sliding* their feet over the pile . . . The handle of the door gave a gentle rattle, and she realised, in a panic, that it was not locked. She never locked her door. Whoever it was who was out there in the tiny hall would find no difficulty in getting in . . . The door began to open slowly, an inch at a time . . . She watched it fearfully, unable to move or cry out, helpless with the fear that gripped her. Wider and wider . . . A figure, shapeless and menacing, loomed in the opening . . . A man in a dark coat with something tied over his face . . . He came slowly and stealthily into the room and moved towards the bed. Inch by inch he covered the strip of carpet between the open door and where she lay . . . Presently he was at the bedside . . . a gloved hand came out slowly and groped towards her . . . the other hand was withdrawn from his pocket, and she saw the knife . . .

And then with a desperate effort she recovered the use of her limbs and, springing up, rolled out of the bed on the other side . . . She heard his muffled, startled cry as she shook herself free of the bed-clothes and gained her feet . . . She saw him coming swiftly toward her, the knife upraised . . . She put up her arms to ward off the blow, and a strangled cry left her parched throat . . . and then he stumbled, almost fell, and clutched at the bed to save himself . . . Jill was past him in a flash, out of the room, and at the front door of the flat. She tore it open and went stumbling frantically down the stairs, her screams echoing and re-echoing through the silent building . . .

3

'Interestin' and peculiar,' murmured Mr. Budd, sleepily. 'You wouldn't be able to recognise this man again. Miss?'

Jill shook her head.

'No,' she answered. 'He had something tied over his face . . . '

'There was nuthin' at all familiar about him — height, build — nuthin' by which you could identify him?' said the stout superintendent.

'No.'

'Pity,' remarked Mr. Budd. He put up a huge hand and concealed a yawn. It was very early, barely six o'clock, and he had come all the way from his house in Streatham when the telephone call from the Yard had reached him. Jill's screams had alarmed the whole block and brought a patrolling policeman in great haste to see what the noise was all about. To him the terrified girl had poured out her incoherent story. The rather sceptical constable had made a thorough search of the flat, and the building, but there was no sign of the night intruder. The window in the kitchen was open and there were muddy marks on the sill and on the polished linoleum of the floor, but that was all that he had left behind him. Jill persuaded the reluctant policeman to telephone to Scotland Yard and the call was relayed to Mr. Budd.

'You say he had a knife?' went on the big man, pursing his lips, 'an' that he was goin' to attack you with it? H'm. It looks as though his object was murder . . . '

'Of course it was murder,' said Jill, with a shudder. 'He came straight over to the bed and pulled the knife out of his pocket. If I'd been asleep . . . '

'It must 'ave been a very nasty experience, Miss,' murmured Mr. Budd, sympathetically. 'It's very queer, too. Why should this feller want to kill you?'

'How should I know?' she retorted, a little crossly.

'Well, that's what I was wonderin', Miss,' he said.

'Do you know any reason why anyone should want to kill you?'

'No,' she declared. 'Of course I don't.'

'There's nuthin' you've been holdin' back, is there?' he asked, suddenly opening his half-closed eyes and gazing at her searchingly.

'Holding back?' She looked at him with a puzzled expression. 'What do you mean?'

'Over this business at Berrydale.' explained Mr. Budd. 'There isn't somethin' that you haven't told us? Somethin' that might be dangerous to the murderer?'

She shook her head.

'No, of course not,' she answered. 'What could there be?'

'You'd know best about that, Miss,' he said.

'There's something I can't remember,' she said, suddenly, 'and it's been worrying me, but it couldn't be that . . . '

'Somethin' you can't remember, Miss?' said Mr. Budd, with interest. 'What exactly do you mean?'

'Well,' she said, 'it was something I saw

in the hall of that house when I found the dead man. Something that wasn't there when we went later . . . '

'What sort o' something?' he asked.

'I don't know,' she replied. 'That's the trouble. I got an impression that something was missing, if you understand what I mean? But I can't imagine what it was. I wish to goodness I could, because I feel that it's important . . . '

'H'm,' remarked the superintendent, thoughtfully. 'It's interestin'. Like havin' the name o' somebody on the tip of your tongue and not bein' able to recollect it.'

'Yes, that expresses it perfectly.'

'Have you told anyone about it?' he inquired.

'Professor Locksley and his nephew, and Mr. Tape,' she answered.

'The feller who was killed was a Greek named Karolides,' he said, suddenly. 'Have you ever heard of him, Miss?'

Again she shook her head.

'No,' she replied. 'How did you identify him?'

'By his fingerprints.' said Mr. Budd,

and yawned widely and long. 'He'd been 'inside' on several occasions . . . '

'You mean in prison?' she asked, and he nodded.

'What had he done?'

'Most things short o' murder,' said Mr. Budd, with a certain amount of exaggeration. 'D'you know Professor Locksley well?'

'Not very,' she answered. 'He's a client of Mr. Tape's and I've seen him once or twice at the office before last night.'

'And Mr. Wayland?'

'I'd never seen him before last night.'

'You went to Berrydale to take Professor Locksley some documents, didn't you?' he inquired.

'Yes.'

'Do you know what they were?'

'No. They were in a sealed envelope. I never saw them.'

They were, she thought, rather getting away from the main object of his visit, which was the mysterious assailant of the night. But Mr. Budd, in spite of his sleepy appearance, appeared to be in a conversational mood. He asked her innumerable questions about herself, and her job; what friends she had, and what sort of man Mr. Tape was to work for. The questions seemed inexhaustible, and many of them he repeated two or three times in a different way. She thought that he was trying to catch her out, and said so. Mr. Budd regarded her with a bland and innocent expression.

'Now would I try an' do a thing like that, Miss?' he said, reproachfully. 'Besides, how could I catch you out if you're tellin' me the truth?'

'You can't, because I am,' she retorted. 'But that doesn't mean you weren't trying.'

'We have to ask all these questions,' he said, deprecatingly. 'It's mostly a matter o' routine. Askin' questions is ninety per cent of all police work.'

He rose with difficulty to take his leave.

'Now don't you go worryin' about anythin',' he said, when she escorted him to the door.

'Supposing this man tries again . . . ?' she began.

'That'll be all right,' he said, reassuringly. 'I'll see that no 'arm comes to you, Miss. Just forget all about it.'

On the doorstep he turned.

'If you should remember this thing that's been botherin' you,' he said, 'will you let me know at once?'

'Of course,' she said, and he went ponderously down the stairs.

When he had gone out of sight, Jill closed the door and, going into the kitchen, began to make herself some breakfast. The adventure of the night had left her a little shaken. Why should the unknown man have tried to kill her? What motive could he possibly have? She puzzled over it while she ate her breakfast, and dressed, but she could find no satisfactory solution.

When she left the flat at a quarter to nine to go to Mr. Tape's office, there was a man lounging in the entrance hall reading a newspaper. He glanced at her quickly as she passed him, and then went on reading his paper. There was another man on the opposite side of the street, smoking a cigarette and looking idly up and down the road. As she walked away he began to stroll leisurely after her. Detectives, she thought. From now on she was going to be watched wherever she went. Mr. Budd was evidently taking no chances . . .

4

The Sacred Ibis occupied the premises of what had, at one time, been a mission hall for seamen. When it had failed to entice a sufficient clientele from the public houses and more dubious entertainments which the district offered, to warrant its remaining open, it was closed, and a firm of furniture manufacturers took it over as a warehouse. Eventually it passed into the hands of Mr. Ahmadun, who had certain structural alterations made to the interior, covered the whitewashed walls with garish murals, secured, by some means known only to himself, a drinking licence, and opened it under the name of The Sacred Ibis Club. The seamen, who had passed it by when it was a mission hall, flocked to it in its new form. It quickly became known that all kinds of entertainment were procurable at The Ibis — illicit and otherwise. It acquired a very bad reputation among the respectable inhabitants of Pennyfields, and the worse its reputation grew, the greater became its clientele. Mr. Ahmadun — if he possessed any other name no one knew of it — waxed fatter and fatter on the profits as the years went by. He was a stout, greasy-looking old man with a long grey beard and a completely bald head, of which, since he invariably wore a dirty red turban, very few people were aware. He lived in a small flat over the club premises, but was more often to be found seated behind a small counter near the entrance, in a high-backed chair, from which point of vantage he could watch everything that went on while he drank innumerable cups of thick, syrupy coffee and smoked strong, yellow cigarettes, which he rolled himself with extraordinary dexterity.

The police had made many raids on the establishment, but they never succeeded in finding anything which offered an excuse for closing it down. Mr. Ahmadun's system of information was very thorough, and on these occasions everything was conducted with scrupulous regard for the regulations. All the same, it became whispered abroad that queer things went on behind the weather-beaten sign of the Ibis which adorned the façade of Mr. Ahmadun's premises; queer and sometimes horrible . . .

A thin white mist had rolled up from the river on the night when Mr. Budd, accompanied by the melancholy Sergeant Leek, elected to pay the place a visit. It was not sufficient to obscure vision to any great extent, but it was enough to make everything damp, clammy and unpleasant. Mr. Ahmadun, sitting in his usual chair, saw them enter the club and pressed his foot on a nail that projected slightly from the floor. In the cellar below, and in several small rooms that opened off the main one, a red light glowed, and there was sudden and immense activity among the occupants . . .

'Do you mind if we come in?' greeted Mr. Budd, who knew Mr. Ahmadun rather well. The old man smiled obsequiously.

'It is a pleasure,' he said, in his soft voice, with its slight accent. 'My poor establishment is pleased to welcome you. If there is anything that I, in my humble way, can do for you, you have only to make your request . . . '

'You were acquainted with a man called Karolides, I think?' said Mr. Budd.

'Karolides? . . . Karolides?' Mr. Ahmadun pursed his lips. 'He has been here once or twice, I believe. I have not seen him for some time . . . '

'You won't see him any more,' said Mr. Budd, curtly. 'He's been murdered.'

Mr. Ahmadun received the news without any outward display of emotion.

'That is very unfortunate,' he murmured.

'I'm looking for a man called Lew Glomm,' continued the big man. 'He knew Karolides . . . '

'I know him,' said Mr. Ahmadun, inclining his head. 'He comes here often, but he is not here tonight. Perhaps he will come later. You think this man Glomm killed Karolides?'

'I've no reason to think so,' answered Mr. Budd. 'I want to ask him a few questions, that's all.'

'I see,' said Mr. Ahmadun. 'You would like to wait and see if he comes in? The hospitality of my poor establishment is yours . . . ' He clapped his hands, and a dark-skinned waiter in a dirty white jacket came hurrying up.

'Conduct these gentlemen to a table,' ordered Mr. Ahmadun, 'and see that they have everything they require. There is to be no charge, you understand?'

The waiter grinned with a wide display of white teeth.

'This way, plizz,' he said, and they followed him across the polished dance floor to a table in a corner near the rostrum, on which a band of four were resting.

'What would you like, sah?' inquired the waiter, and Mr. Budd ordered beer for himself and coffee for Leek, who was a teetotaller.

'Seems a pleasant old bloke, the boss of this place,' remarked the sergeant, when the waiter had gone, and Mr. Budd grunted.

'He'd slit the throats of all his family for sixpence,' he said. 'That's just 'ow pleasant 'e is! Don't you make no mistake about Ahmadun. He's one o' the most dangerous crooks alive, an' he's so cunning that nobody can hang anythin' on 'im.'

He looked sleepily round the place. It was not very full as yet, but there was a fair number there all the same, for the premises were large. They were a mixed crowd of all nationalities, with a good sprinkling of flashy-looking women. The band began to play a very hot swing number and the floor became alive with dancers. The music was harsh and savage, but it blended very well with the general atmosphere of the place. These people were half savages, too. Their emotions were primitive and uncivilised, and the music, which had come, via America, from the African jungle, appealed to them. The frenzied blowing of the trumpet and the ryhthm of the drums had as much power over their senses, here, as it had had in its original form, at the negro orgies to which it owed its inception. It required very little effort of the imagination to change these people, wildly jitterbugging, to painted, half-naked savages capering madly round a smoky fire to the shrill chanting of the witch doctors . . .

Civilisation was on the down grade, thought Mr. Budd, as he watched. It had reached its peak many years ago, and was now declining rapidly. The graciousness had gone out of life, and of people. It, and they, were becoming harsh and discordant, like the music to which they danced. Good manners and behaviour were an exception these days. The world was like a lovely garden that was being overrun and choked with weeds . . . Progress . . . but in which direction? There was only one answer to *that* if you compared the rowdy, noisy present with the melodious graciousness of the past. The whole population seemed to be sliding, fighting and kicking and screaming in their haste to get there, into a great, yawning pit which they themselves had dug . . .

A man had come in and was talking to Mr. Ahmadun. He was short and thin, dressed smartly in a suit of a rather loud check. He was looking over at them, and Mr. Budd recognised him at once. It was Lew Glomm.

Presently he threaded his way through the dancers and up to their table.

'Hello, Lew,' greeted Mr. Budd, genially. 'Sit down an' 'ave a drink.'

'What jer want?' grunted Mr. Glomm. his small eyes full of suspicion and wariness. ''E says you was lookin' fer me . . . '

'Quite right, Lew,' said Mr. Budd. 'I came 'ere specially to see you. Now sit down . . . '

'What d'you want with me?' demanded Lew Glomm. 'You've got nuthin' on me. I'm goin' straight, I am . . . '

'I'm sure you are,' said the big man. 'I've got nuthin' on you, Lew, as you say. 'An I don't want to 'ave anythin' on yer. All I want is a little information . . . '

'What about?'

'Sit down an' I'll tell you,' said Mr. Budd.

Mr. Glomm hesitated, looked quickly round, and then reluctantly seated himself.

'I got a date,' he said. 'I can't stay long . . . '

'Long enough,' murmured Mr. Budd. 'Long enough, I'm sure, Lew. What'll you have?'

'I don't want nuthin',' said Mr. Glomm. 'Tell me what yer want, and get it over with. I got ter see someone on business . . . '

'Gone into business, 'ave yer, Lew?' remarked Mr. Budd. 'An' doin' pretty well by the look of you.' His eyes rested thoughtfully on the diamond that sparkled on Mr. Glomm's little finger. 'I'll bet that cost quite a bit . . . '

'Never you mind what it cost,' snapped Lew, ungraciously.

'I'm only interested, Lew,' said Mr. Budd. 'I'm always pleased to see a feller get on . . . '

'Cut all the frills an get down to brass tacks,' said Lew. 'What d'yer want?'

'You know a man called Karolides,' said Mr. Budd. 'I want to know all you can tell me about him.' The gentle, bantering tone of his voice had changed. It was curt and businesslike.

'I don't know nuthin' about him,' said Lew Glomm.

'Oh, come now, Lew,' began Mr. Budd.

'I tell yer I don't know nuthin',' said Lew. 'If yer wants to know anythin', why don't yer go an' ask him himself?'

'Because he's dead, Lew,' answered Mr. Budd, gently. 'He was murdered. You know that very well . . . '

'Me?' cried Lew. ' 'Ow should I know . . . ?'

'Because Ahmadun told you when you came in,' murmured the big man. 'So just come clean, Lew, an' tell me all you know about Karolides.'

'I tell yer I don't know nuthin',' said Lew, obstinately.

Mr. Budd sighed.

'I don't want ter get unpleasant,' he said, 'unless you force me to. This is a serious business, Lew. Karolides had his head bashed in . . . '

'Well, you can't pin it on me,' said Glomm, quickly. 'I've got an alibi . . . '

'Have you now?' said Mr. Budd. 'Well, well, now isn't that remarkable? If you didn't know he was dead or *when* he died, how can you have an alibi, Lew? Or have you got a permanent alibi?'

Mr. Glomm realised his mistake and was silent.

'You knew he was dead, an' how he died, and when he died,' continued Mr. Budd. 'So let's have it, Lew.'

Lew licked his lips and leaned across the table earnestly.

'Look 'ere,' he said, in a low voice. 'I'll admit I knew Karolides, an' that he was dead. But I swear I had nuthin' to do with it. I ... I just 'eard about it, that's all ... '

'Go on,' said Mr. Budd, as he stopped. 'Give me the rest of it, Lew.'

'I can't talk 'ere,' whispered Lew, looking round, 'an' I've got ter meet this feller. 'E'll be 'ere in a few minutes. Come round to my digs — 10 Lamb Street, just off the causeway. Wait until I leave 'ere, and then pop along ... '

'All right,' agreed Mr Budd 'Don't go tryin' any tricks though, Lew, or I'll 'ave yer pulled in ... '

'Yer needn't worry,' said Lew. 'I'll be glad ter get this off me chest. I'm a bit scared, to tell yer the truth ... '

'Scared?' said Mr. Budd.. 'What are yer scared of. Lew?'

'Of . . . ' Lew Glomm broke off. 'There's the fellow I got to see,' he said, hurriedly, and getting up quickly, he went to join the man who had just come in . . .

5

He was tall and wore a light, fawn-coloured raincoat. When he took off the soft-brimmed hat he was wearing, Mr. Budd saw that he was quite young and fairly good-looking. He was not at all the type of man that might be expected to come to a place like The Sacred Ibis, or to have any interest in a man like Lew Glomm.

Mr. Budd lit one of his thin black cigars and, leaning back in his chair, watched them sleepily through the evil-smelling smoke . . . Lew had taken the newcomer to an isolated table, and they were in deep and earnest conversation. Some fiddle going on for somebody, thought the big man, and wondered what Lew had meant when he said he was scared. What was he scared about? And what was he anxious to get off his chest? Something about the murder; that would probably be it. Like all his class, Lew

Glomm would be scared of getting mixed up with the Big Thing. He knew something, and he was going to make a clean breast of it, so that there could be nothing coming back on him. Mr. Budd called the waiter and ordered more beer.

'What about you?' he remarked to the melancholy Leek. 'Goin' ter have some more coffee?'

The sergeant shook his head.

'No, I don't like the stuff they make 'ere,' he said. 'Too thick an' treacly for my taste.' He waited until the waiter was out of earshot and then went on: 'Who d'you think that feller is with Glomm?'

'I've no idea,' said Mr. Budd. 'Looks quite a respectable sort o' feller, don't he?'

'That's what I was thinkin',' said Leek. 'You never can tell, though. 'E may be one o' these West End jewel thieves . . . Hello, where's old Ahmadun gone to?'

The high-backed chair was empty. Mr. Ahmadun had slipped away somewhere. The stout superintendent blew out a cloud of smoke.

'Gone up to his flat, most likely,' he said, and yawned. 'I shall be glad when we can get away from 'ere. I'm getting a bit tired. I didn't have much sleep last night an' the night before.'

'It's a funny thing' said the sergeant, 'but I'm tired meself . . . '

'There's nuthin' funny about that,' said Mr. Budd. 'It's just your natural state . . . '

'I often think there must be somethin' wrong with me . . . ' began Leek, lugubriously.

'I don't think — I'm sure of it,' said Mr. Budd, unkindly.

'What I mean is, I ought ter see a doctor,' explained the sergeant. 'I never get really merry and bright these days . . . '

'Did you ever?' demanded his superior. 'I've never seen you lookin' like anythin' but a mute at a funeral.'

'When I was a boy,' said Leek, sadly, 'they used ter call me 'little mischief' . . . '

'I'll bet that wasn't the only thing they called yer,' snarled Mr. Budd.

'Me mother used to say I was 'er little ray of sunshine,' said the sergeant, reminiscently.

'You must 'ave suffered a total eclipse since then,' said Mr. Budd. 'What did yer father call yer?'

'He was always making jokes,' said Leek. ''E said I was the only really effective argument ever put up for birth control. Always makin' us laugh 'e was . . .'

'If he ever succeeded in makin' *you* laugh, he must have bin a wonderful man,' remarked Mr. Budd 'Here's Ahmadun back again.'

The sergeant raised his eyes. Mr. Ahmadun had just appeared through a curtained archway at the back of his chair, and was preparing to resume his seat. Almost at the same moment, Lew Glomm and the man in the light raincoat got up and began to move towards the entrance.

'They're off,' said Mr. Budd, with satisfaction. 'We'll give 'em a few minutes an' then we'll go an' find Lamb Street . . .'

Lew Glomm paused to say something to Mr. Ahmadun, and then left the club with his companion. The big man waited nearly fifteen minutes and then he rose ponderously to his feet and lumbered across the dance floor with Leek at his heels. The band was resting and the floor was clear of dancers, so that Mr. Ahmadun had no difficulty in seeing them approach from his chair near the entrance. His eyes regarded them paternally, and he raised his right hand and gently stroked his beard.

Mr. Budd, whose deceptively sleepy-looking eyes missed nothing, saw the apparently innocent action and began to think. They reached the little counter, and he paused. From the corner of his eye he had seen three men get up quietly and go out through a narrow door marked 'Private,' and this had immediately followed Mr. Ahmadun's beard stroking.

'You are going?' said Mr. Ahmadun, softly.

'Yes,' answered Mr. Budd, shortly.

'I hope,' said Ahmadun, 'that your visit has been of advantage and that you had everything you wanted . . . '

'Yes, thank you,' murmured the big man. He was thinking rapidly. The suave old devil in the chair was up to something . . .

'My poor establishment is always at your service,' went on Mr. Ahmadun. 'I hope that you will come again . . . '

'May I use your telephone?' asked Mr. Budd, suddenly. The instrument stood on the counter close to Mr. Ahmadun's hand.

'Certainly,' said the old man, but he looked a little disconcerted.

Mr. Budd dialled a number.

'Hello,' he said, when the connection was made. 'That the police station? I want to speak to the inspector in charge . . . Sup'n'endent Budd, C.I.D. New Scotland Yard . . . Evenin', Inspector. I'm at The Sacred Ibis . . . No, no trouble. Just payin' a visit, that's all. But you know what this district's like? . . . Well, maybe worse than that . . . I'm just leaving, an' I thought you might send a couple o' men along to see that I don't come to any harm . . . Yes, in about ten minutes . . . Thank you.'

Mr. Budd hung up the receiver and looked sleepily at Mr. Ahmadun.

'Nuthin' like takin' precautions,' he said. 'Of course, I don't s'pose there's anythin' likely to 'appen, but yer never know, do yer? These parts are pretty rough, an' fellers in my profession ain't too popular . . . '

'No, no,' said Mr. Ahmadun. 'A . . . a very wise precaution . . . ' He appeared to be rather flurried. His usual calm had deserted him, and there was a glint of fury in his eyes.

'Of course,' said Mr. Budd, imperturbably, 'we're safe enough 'ere. You'd see that nuthin' 'appened to us 'ere, but outside it's a different matter . . . '

'Yes, yes, of course,' muttered the old man. He looked round anxiously and beckoned to a waiter. The man came hastily, and Mr. Ahmadun whispered something in his ear. He nodded and hurried away, passing out through the door which the three men had previously made their exit. Mr. Budd's stolid face never moved a muscle, but he had seen and noted what had taken place, and felt that his telephone call had not been wasted.

'Yes,' said Mr. Ahmadun, and he was once again his placid self, 'it is a dangerous district for strangers. Many unpleasant things happen. It would grieve me if anything happened to you . . . '

'I'm sure it would,' murmured Mr. Budd. 'It'd grieve me, too.' He lit a cigar and looked lazily round. The band had started another dance tune and the floor was full. The waiter came back through the side door and nodded to Mr. Ahmadun.

'Well,' remarked the big man, 'I think we may as well be goin' now.'

'I trust that you will come again,' said Mr. Ahmadun, softly. 'You will always be welcome . . . '

He watched them as they went out, and there was sheer, naked hate in his eyes . . .

6

'Why d'jer phone up the 'nick' for those men?' asked Leek, as they stood outside the club in the damp white mist, which had thickened. 'Was you expectin' trouble?'

'I think I was,' said Mr. Budd, peering about. 'I had a sudden hunch. An' there was *goin'* ter be trouble — big trouble . . . H'm, there they are . . . '

Leek followed the direction of his eyes and saw a shadowy group of men standing on the corner of the street a few yards away.

'That door must be another exit to the place,' murmured Mr. Budd, almost to himself. 'The old devil! He must 'ave arranged for them fellers to slip out just before we left and wait fer us . . . If I hadn't put that call through, I don't think we'd 'ave ever reached Lamb Street, or anywhere else . . . '

'Do you mean . . . ?' began the sergeant, incredulously.

'Yes, all that an' more,' grunted Mr. Budd. 'Now don't start askin' questions. 'Ere comes the police . . . '

Two uniformed men loomed out of the thin fog, and the big man hailed them.

'It's all right, boys,' he said, when he had shown them his warrant card. 'I don't think there's any danger now . . . ' He glanced in the direction of the place where the three men had been lurking, but they were no longer there. 'The wolves 'ave gone.'

'Wolves is right, sir,' said one of the constables. 'Some of 'em round 'ere's more like wild animals than 'uman bein's. The worst of the lot's that Ahmadun what runs The Ibis. 'E's an old b — 'e is.'

'I couldn't 'ave put it better meself,' said Mr. Budd. 'How far is Lamb Street from ere?'

'Take the first turnin' on the right an' that brings you out on the Causeway,' said the other policeman. 'It's the secon' turnin' on the left . . . '

'Pretty 'ot neighbourhood, sir,' broke in the first constable. ''Adn't we better come along with yer?'

The big man considered for a moment. It might be useful to have the men handy. If Lew Glomm was playing any tricks . . .

'Yes,' he said. 'You come along as far as the end of the street, an' then 'ang about until I come back. I've got a call ter make on a feller who might 'ave some information I want . . . ' He explained briefly as they walked away.

The streets seemed to be deserted, but every now and again they caught a glimpse of furtive figures lurking in doorways and the mouths of alleys. They appeared to melt away into the misty gloom in some mysterious way as they approached, leaving no trace that they had ever existed. In the better lighted Causeway there was more life. Traffic was rumbling back and forth, slowly on account of the mist, and there were people hurrying along the pavements. They came to Lamb Street, a narrow road with two rows of dilapidated houses, and halted.

'Give us an hour,' said Mr. Budd. 'If we ain't back by then, come along to No. 10 an' find us.'

He turned into the evil-smelling street, accompanied by Leek, and sought for No. 10. After some difficulty he found it: a dreary-looking building that differed not at all from its dreary-looking neighbours. There were no front gardens to the houses in Lamb Street. The front doors opened directly on to the narrow and broken pavement. Mr. Budd surveyed the outside of the house without enthusiasm. It was quite dark. There was not a glimmer of light showing from any of the flat windows. In the middle of the blistered door was a knocker of rusty iron and he used it, beating a soft tattoo. He thought he heard a faint sound from behind the closed door, rather like a smothered gasp, but nothing happened. Nobody came to answer his summons. After a pause he knocked again, more loudly. This time there was no sound at all — the house remained completely and utterly silent.

'Looks as though there wasn't nobody in,' remarked Leek, and Mr. Budd grunted.

'Does, doesn't it?' he said. 'Maybe Glomm ain't got back yet, but I'll swear I 'eard somebody inside just now . . . '

'I never 'eard anythin',' said the sergeant. 'What do we do now?'

'We'll wait fer a bit,' said the stout superintendent. 'I . . . ' He broke off suddenly. Accidentally he had pressed against the door and it was opening. He pushed it wider and peered into the darkness of the hall, listening. He could hear nothing. Out of the darkness came a smell of dirt and ancient cooking: a thick, heavy smell that hung in the air as though it had been collecting for years, as indeed it probably had. He waited a second or two, and then he stepped into the narrow passage beyond the door and struck a match. When it flared up he saw a rickety hall table, a patch of threadbare linoleum, and some coats and hats hanging from nails driven into the wall. Beside the table was a door, evidently leading into the ground-floor room, and beyond that a flight of stairs.

'Anyone at home?' His voice boomed and echoed through the house, but nobody answered him.

'Queer,' he murmured. 'Surely there must be *somebody* 'ere.'

The match burned down to his fingers and he dropped it, stamping out the charred remains, and lit another. There was an unshaded electric light bulb hanging on a flex from the ceiling, and he looked round for a switch. He found it half-hidden by a man's coat, and pressed it down. The light came on, but the bulb was a low-powered one and very dirty, and the illumination it gave was not very brilliant. It was better than striking matches, however. Mr. Budd rubbed his chin and considered.

'I think we'd better 'ave a look round,' he said at last. 'It seems funny to me that the door should be open an' nobody at home.' He looked at the latch. The catch had been pushed up. 'H'm,' he continued, thoughtfully. 'Maybe someone's slipped out for a moment. P'raps we'd better 'ang on fer a bit before we do anythin' further.'

'I should 'ave thought . . . ' began Leek, and stopped. A sound interrupted him, and it came from behind the closed door beside the hall table. It was half a groan and half a sigh, and was followed by a confused muttering.

'There's someone in there,' said Mr. Budd, and moved over to the door and turned the handle. It was unlocked, and he pushed it open cautiously. The room was in darkness, but the light from the hall lit it up sufficiently for him to be able to see that it was full of odd bits of furniture and indescribably untidy. There was an old, broken-down divan bed in one corner, and on this, fully dressed, lay a fat woman. Her bloated red face was smeared with dirt, and her hair straggled in thin wisps all over it. There was an empty bottle on the floor and an overturned glass. Mr. Budd sniffed the air, which was heavy with the fumes of spirit . . .

'Drunk,' he said, going over and staring down at the woman. 'Dead to the world.' He stooped and picked up the bottle. 'Gin,' he remarked. 'H'm, well, that's why she didn't come to the door when we knocked. Looks as if she was the landlady . . . '

The woman groaned and stirred uneasily.

'Don't look as though she'd recover until the morning,' said Mr. Budd. He came quietly out and shut the door. 'What can 'ave happened to Glomm? 'E ought to be back by now . . . '

'P'raps 'e never meant ter come back,' suggested Leek. 'Maybe 'e's got scared an' 'opped it . . . '

''E'd never be so silly,' said Mr. Budd, but there was doubt in his voice all the same. ''E knows he couldn't get far, an' I told him if he tried any tricks I'd pull him in . . . '

'If 'e'd 'ad anythin' ter do with this Greek feller's murder, 'e'd risk it,' said Leek, not without a certain amount of sense.

Mr. Budd pulled irritably at a fold of loose flesh beneath his chin.

'I never thought 'e'd be such a fool,' he muttered, crossly.

'You don't know 'ow far he may be mixed up in it,' said the sergeant. 'P'raps he killed the feller himself . . . '

The big man shook his head.

'I'm pretty sure 'e didn't,' he declared,

with conviction. 'Lew wouldn't have anything to do with murder — not if he knew about it. He's mixed up in it all right, but somebody else killed Karolides, an' that's why 'e's scared. Maybe 'e's tryin' to get rid of that young feller 'e was with . . .'

They waited, but Mr. Glomm did not put in an appearance. At the end of half an hour, the impatient Mr. Budd came to a decision.

'You wait 'ere,' he said to Leek. 'I'm goin' to have a look at his room upstairs. Maybe I'll find something interestin' before 'e comes, if he's coming.'

The weary Leek nodded gloomily, and the big man went up the stairs. He moved very softly for his bulk, and reached the front landing without any more noise than a protesting creak from the stair treads. A window faced him, and on his right was a closed door. He tried it, expecting to find that it was locked, but it opened when he turned the handle. He found himself in a room that was directly over the one downstairs in which the stout woman lay in her drunken stupor. It was pitch dark, and he fumbled round the door frame to find the switch. His groping fingers found it, and he pressed it down . . .

Leek was staring out into the street when Mr. Budd rejoined him softly.

'Well,' he asked, 'did yer find anythin'?'

'I found Lew Glomm,' answered the big man, grimly.

'What, 'as 'e been 'ere all the time?' exclaimed the sergeant. 'Well, would yer believe it? Was 'e asleep . . . ?'

'He's dead,' snapped Mr. Budd, curtly. 'He's lyin' up in his room with a knife stuck in his back. Go an' tell those fellers to come 'ere at once an' then telephone the station an' notify them what's 'appened . . . '

'Dead!' gasped Leek. 'Murdered! Who . . .'

'I don't know who,' snarled Mr. Budd. 'But I'm circulatin' a description of that young feller in the light coat Glomm was with at The Sacred Ibis, an' 'avin' 'im pulled in. Now, don't stand there gapin'. Get a move on . . . '

7

The squalid little street became full of activity half an hour later that night. The news of the crime at No. 10 had seeped through to the other residents of Lamb Street, and they had turned out of their houses, in various stages of undress, to join in the free entertainment that had come their way. Murder was not uncommon in that neighbourhood, but it never failed to provide a thrill, and the sightseers stared with fascinated eyes at the two police cars drawn up by the kerb. The stolid constable on guard at the door of No. 10 could hear the whispers, like wind through a cornfield, that ran up and down the street.

Inside the house, up in Lew Glomm's room, the divisional surgeon, roused hastily from his bed, and in consequence rather bad-tempered, was making his examination, while Mr. Budd and the Divisional Inspector waited for his report.

Downstairs, in the room below, a policeman was trying, with the aid of cold water and hot coffee, to rouse the fat woman from her stupor. In the narrow hall the photographers and fingerprint men waited to be called.

'The knife severed the aorta,' grunted the doctor, getting to his feet. 'The blow must have been delivered by somebody who was fairly muscular, and this man died practically at once. That's all I can tell you, except that death took place within two hours from now. That would be round eleven-thirty. I can't be more accurate than that. You can move him when you like. I'm going back to bed now, but I'll be ready to do the post-mortem in the morning . . . ' He picked up his bag. 'Why the hell do all these people have to be killed in the middle of the night?' he grumbled, and with a curt nod went clattering down the stairs. His place was taken almost at once by the photographers and the fingerprint experts. The pop and flare of magnesium powder went on for ten minutes, and then the photographers packed up their paraphernalia.

'All right, George, you can have it all,' he said, cheerfully, and his companion went to work. He started on the handle of the knife, and shook his head at the result.

'I'm wasting me time here,' he said. 'The murderer wore gloves.'

'They all do, these days,' grunted the inspector. 'It's these crime books . . . '

'It doesn't make any difference, we still catch 'em,' said George, working busily on the door handle. 'You'd think they'd realise that by now, wouldn't you?'

'It's vanity,' remarked Mr. Budd, with a prodigious yawn. 'They all think that they are the clever ones. That they're not going to make no mistakes — not like Tom, Dick, or Harry . . . '

'And they make 'em all the time.' George began to whistle a popular dance tune softly. 'There's prints here, but they're probably the dead man's . . . '

He finished at last, and Mr. Budd and the Inspector were left alone. The big man looked sleepily round the disordered room.

'He was lookin' for something,' he said.

''E's turned the place upside down. I wonder if he found what he was lookin' for?'

'We'll soon know,' said the inspector confidently.

'That description's gone out to all stations and patrols. He'll be pulled in before mornin', I'll bet.' He went over to the door and called down the stairs: 'Jackson!'

'Sir?' answered a voice.

'Is that woman coming round?'

'Not yet, sir, but I don't think it'll be long.'

'I hope not,' grunted the inspector. 'Well,' he came back and looked at the sprawling figure of Mr. Glomm, 'we may as well have *that* taken away . . . '

Mr. Budd nodded in agreement. The body had been searched and they had found nothing that was helpful. Two men with a stretcher came in and all that was left of Lew Glomm was carried with difficulty down the narrow stairs and out to the ambulance, which had just arrived.

'Now we'll go through this litter,' said Mr. Budd. 'Give us a hand, Leek.'

The sergeant, who had been leaning against the door, watching wearily, came reluctantly forward.

'I'm sorry to disturb your beauty sleep,' said Mr. Budd, sarcastically. 'I was beginnin' to wonder which was the corpse.' He set to work methodically to make a thorough search of the room. It took some time, with even the three of them, and when they had finished Mr. Budd mopped his perspiring face.

'Well, that's that,' he said, disappointedly. 'Nuth'n'.'

'What did you expect to find?' asked the inspector.

The big man shook his head.

'I dunno,' he replied. 'Somethin' that'd link up the killin' of Glomm with the murder of Karolides an' the attempted murder o' Miss Hartley. Somebody's bein' very busy at homicide, an' they ain't doin' it fer fun. There's a reason for it . . .'

'Well, in Glomm's case the reason's pretty easy,' said the inspector. 'He was going to talk . . .'

'But what was he goin' ter talk *about*?'

murmured Mr. Budd. 'An' *who* was 'e goin' ter talk about?'

'This man we're looking for — the young feller in the light-coloured rain-coat,' said the inspector.

'Maybe,' Mr. Budd pursed his lips and gazed at a corner of the ceiling. 'Yes, maybe that's who 'e was goin' ter talk about, an' then again maybe it wasn't.'

The inspector looked at him sharply. Really, he thought, it was remarkable how these fellers got into the C.I.D. at Headquarters.

The was a tap on the door and a constable put in his head.

'Excuse me, sir,' he said to the inspector, 'but Mrs. Grice is round.'

'Mrs. Grice? . . . Oh, the woman downstairs. All right, I'll come at once,' said the inspector.

'I'll come with yer,' said Mr. Budd. 'You stay 'ere, Leek, an' don't go 'avin' a sleep . . . ' He was gone before the aggrieved sergeant could reply.

Mrs. Grice was sitting on the edge of the ramshackle divan looking very sorry for herself. Her hair was wet and hung in ratstails round her face, and her eyes were heavy and bloodshot. She was conscious, but that was about all. She was swaying back and forth and moaning discordantly. As Mr. Budd and the inspector came into the room, she looked up and eyed them blearily.

'Wass goin' on?' she muttered with difficulty. 'Washcr all doin' in my 'ouse, eh? Wass goin' on . . . ?'

'Murder has been goin' on,' said Mr. Budd. 'Your lodger, Lew Glomm, has been killed . . . '

'Good riddance,' said the woman thickly. 'Go 'way, all of yer. I wanter go sleep . . . ' She attempted to lie down, but the constable caught her shoulders and pulled her up.

'Come now, Ma,' he said. 'You can't go to sleep yet . . . '

She broke into a string of foul language — a stream of invective that would have shamed a bargee.

'That'll do,' snapped Mr. Budd, curtly. 'Now, pull yerself together. Give 'er more coffee, will yer.'

The other policeman poured out a cup

from a jug on the table.

'Come on, drink this,' he said. She tried to push the cup away, but he held it to her lips firmly. It slopped all over her, running down her chin and neck, but she swallowed some of it and gasped and spluttered.

'Why don' yer lemme alone?' she muttered. 'Wanner go to sleep . . . '

'Walk her about,' said the inspector. 'She's still very drunk.'

The two policemen hoisted her to her feet and, supporting her between them, began to walk her up and down the room. She sagged between them like a sack and swore incoherently.

'It'll be some time before she's in a fit state to answer questions,' grunted Mr. Budd, in disgust. 'We may as well . . . ' He was interrupted by Leek's voice from upstairs.

'I say,' called the sergeant. 'There's a queer thing up 'ere . . . '

'I know, *you're* up there,' snarled Mr. Budd, who was weary and irritable. 'What is it?'

'I've found somethin',' answered Leek.

'Come along up an' see . . . '

The big man mounted the stairs, followed by the inspector. Leek was hovering in the doorway of Lew Glomm's room excitedly.

'What is it? What 'ave yer found?' demanded Mr. Budd.

'I thought I'd 'ave another look in case we'd missed anythin',' explained the lean sergeant, 'an' I found that.' He stabbed a forefinger toward the floor. The threadbare carpet had been turned back at one corner, and a portion of a floorboard had been lifted out, disclosing a cavity.

'Wait till yer see what's inside,' said Leek, complacently, and led the way over.

Mr. Budd peered down into the oblong hole and his fat face puckered thoughtfully. It contained a lamp: a queer-shaped lamp such as he had never seen before. It was made of some metal that looked like silver, and was badly tarnished, but this did not detract from the delicate workmanship.

''Member that bit o' paper you found

under Karolides?' said Leek. 'The Seven Lamps . . . ?'

'Yes,' grunted Mr. Budd. 'But this is only *one* Lamp. If this is one o' the seven, where are the other six?'

PART FOUR

THE MAN FROM AMERICA

1

Professor Locksley frowned at the lamp that stood on his blotting pad and gently rubbed his high forehead.

'It is an imitation of early Persian workmanship,' he declared. 'The metal from which it is made is antimony, not silver, as you suggested, and in my opinion it has very little value.'

'It couldn't 'ave anything to do with these Seven Lamps you was telling me about?' said Mr. Budd, and Locksley shook his head.

'Nothing whatever,' he affirmed. 'The period is wrong, the workmanship is wrong — you can see that it is comparatively modern — and the material is wrong. No, this can have nothing whatever to do with the legendary Lamps of the Gods.'

Mr. Budd sighed and caressed his ample chins. He had brought the lamp, which Leek had discovered under the floorboard in Lew Glomm's room, to Locksley with high hopes, and the Professor's verdict had dashed these to the ground.

'The Seven Lamps of which I spoke,' said Locksley, 'have, as I told you then, never, to my knowledge, been discovered. There is a certain amount of doubt as to whether they ever existed.'

'In fact,' said Mr. Budd, 'that scrap of paper which was found under the body of Karolides may not have referred to *your* Seven Lamps at all?'

'Quite possibly not,' agreed Locksley. 'Very probably not. It was only a theory of mine, you will remember. The words 'Seven Lamps' struck a chord in my memory, and I at once recollected that passage in the translation of the Holling papyrus. But . . . ' he shrugged his stooping shoulders, 'there is nothing to show that it has any connection with this murder, or rather I should say murders. This lamp might be worth two or three pounds, but certainly not more. As a motive for murder it would seem a little inadequate.'

The big man nodded.

'I can't understand why he should 'ave taken the trouble to hide it, if it had no value,' he said, thoughtfully. 'Seems a stupid thing ter do . . . '

'Perhaps he thought it *was* valuable,' replied Professor Locksley. 'People get erroneous ideas about the value of an article, and to the uninitiated this would have the appearance . . . '

'Maybe you're right, sir,' said Mr. Budd, but privately he didn't think anything of the sort. The lamp might not be valuable in itself, but it stood for something that was. Karolides had died because of it, and because of six others. The scrap of paper had mentioned seven lamps, and it was too much of a coincidence to believe that this lamp was not one of the seven referred to. Karolides had died, and so had Lew Glomm, and they had definitely not been killed for an imitation antique.

And in some way there was a thread connecting their deaths with Professor Locksley. Karolides had thought, when he came to Berrydale on that foggy night, that he was going to Locksley's house . . . Locksley might not know anything about it, but he was definitely mixed up in it somewhere. It was a puzzler. He felt like a man floundering about in the dark in unfamiliar country . . .

'Well, sir,' he said, getting ponderously to his feet, 'I'm very sorry to have troubled you, but I thought you might be able to help us.'

'No trouble at all,' said Locksley, pleasantly. 'I'm infinitely obliged to you, Superintendent. This business, I must admit, intrigues me. I have never come in close contact with murder before, or heard of one with such unusual features.'

'Unusual is right, sir,' said Mr. Budd, packing up the lamp and putting it back in the cardboard box in which he had brought it. 'What gets over me is why this feller Karolides was comin' to see you that night. I s'pose you haven't been able to think of a reason?'

'No,' said Locksley, 'and I've thought about it a good deal, I can assure you. I've never heard of the man before. Why he should have been coming to see me I can't imagine . . . '

There was a tap at the door and Mrs. Moule came in.

'There's a young lady wishes to see you, sir,' she said. 'A Miss Karina.'

'Karina? . . . A young lady?' Professor Locksley pursed his lips and his bushy brows drew together. 'What — er — does she want?'

'I understand it is in connection with your book, sir,' said the housekeeper.

'In connection with my book?' repeated Locksley. 'Dear me, this is very extraordinary. A young lady in connection with my book? Well, well, perhaps I had better see her, Mrs. Moule. Ask her to wait a few minutes and then show her up.'

The housekeeper withdrew, and Mr Budd prepared to take his departure.

'If there's anything that I can do to — er — help at any time,' said Professor Locksley, as he said goodbye, 'please don't hesitate to come and ask me. As I said, I am very interested — very interested, indeed.'

Mr. Budd saw the visitor waiting in the hall as he went out. She looked foreign, he thought, and very expensively dressed; rather pretty in a way . . . He took note of her automatically, but without much interest. Later he was to be very interested indeed.

2

He went back to the Yard, made his way to his cheerless office, and settled himself behind his desk. He was very tired. It had been in the early hours of the morning before he had got home, and there had been barely time to snatch a couple of hours' sleep before he was up and about again. Weariness and disappointment made him feel irritable and depressed. He had hoped that the lamp would provide a valuable clue, and it had done nothing of the sort. It had only made things more difficult. Lighting a cigar, he leaned back in his chair, clasped his hands across his capacious stomach and, closing his eyes, tried to think.

When Mrs. Grice had eventually recovered sufficiently to be able to talk coherently, she had not been able to add very much to his slender stock of knowledge. She knew very little about Glomm. He had been living there for quite a considerable time and always paid up regularly. He was quiet and had few visitors. He was the only lodger she had at present — times were very bad. On the night of the murder she had gone out earlier in the evening to *The Grape Vine*, a public house which she was in the habit of frequenting. Over a few drinks she had struck up an acquaintance with a man — a complete stranger whom she had never seen before. He had given a her a bottle of gin and walked home with her as far as her door. She was, she admitted, a bit 'fuddled' even then — she had had trouble with her key, and he had opened the door for her. When she got in she went straight to her room and opened the gin. That was all she remembered. Whether the stranger had given her back her key or not she couldn't tell, but when she searched her bag, at Mr. Budd's request, it was not there. She gave a hazy description of the man she had met, but it was of little value since it might have fitted almost anyone. He was fairly young and had a moustache which she thought was dark, but wasn't sure.

It was quite obvious that the meeting, and the present of the gin, had been planned by the murderer. It had been quite a clever way of gaining admittance to the house and ensuring that Mrs. Grice would not be in a state to interfere in anything that might happen. It could have been carried out by the man in the fawn raincoat before he had come to meet Lew Glomm at The Sacred Ibis. Well, they ought to be hearing something about him pretty soon. At any moment he might be pulled in and, maybe, what he would have to say would be interesting. It was next to impossible to work out any sort of a theory at present. There wasn't enough to go on.

He began to arrange the actual facts in his possession. Karolides, a well-known crook and suspected fence, had been on his way to see Professor Locksley, a noted authority on ancient Egypt, when he had been tricked into entering an empty house instead and had there been murdered. The murder had been discovered by Jill Hartley, secretary to a firm of solicitors, Messrs. Tape, Redman and

Tape, who had come to Berrydale with some documents for Locksley, and accidentally fallen into the same trap which the murderer had set for Karolides. She had seen something in the hall of the empty house which had gone when she returned with the police later, but she couldn't remember what it was. Under the body of Karolides had been found a scrap of paper bearing the words 'Seven Lamps.' Professor Locksley had suggested that they referred to a legend contained in the translation of a 5,000-year-old papyrus about the Lamps of the Gods. A search of Karolides' rooms had brought to light a portion of a letter from a man named Lew Glomm, also a known crook, making an appointment at a dubious East End club called The Sacred Ibis, and run by a man known as Mr. Ahmadun. An attack had been made on the girl, Jill Hartley, by an unknown man who had broken into her flat in the middle of the night and tried to stab her with a knife, for no apparent reason, unless he had been afraid that she knew something, dangerous to his safety, about the murder of

Karolides. A visit to The Sacred Ibis had resulted in contacting Lew Glomm, who had said that he was scared and made an appointment for later on at his lodgings. He had had an appointment with a man in a light-coloured raincoat, whom he met at the club and with whom he had left. Mr. Ahmadun had attempted to arrange an ambush outside the club which had been unsuccsessful, but which showed that he had some reason to fear them, i.e., himself and Leek. They had gone to keep the appointment with Glomm, and found that he had been killed. In a space under the floorboards they had found a lamp, which turned out to be an imitation antique of no particular value at all.

That, thought Mr. Budd, was a pretty good summary of events, and that was practically all he had to work on. It was, when you came to think about it seriously, not very much. But, all the same, there might be something to be extracted from it. He shifted into a more comfortable position and put his feet up on the desk. The trick of the name boards at Berrydale and the trick of the gin with

Mrs. Grice seemed to suggest that the same person had been responsible in both cases. The same *type* of mind had been at work. The whole question was — why? What had been the motive for the murders? Fear? Gain? Which? What had this man been afraid of, or what had he expected to gain? What lay at the back of it all? Something pretty big, evidently. A man doesn't commit murder for nothing . . .

The ringing of the telephone bell broke in on his cogitations. Stretching out his hand, he picked up the receiver and held it to his ear.

'Call for you, sir.' said the switchboard operator. 'Professor Locksley . . . '

'Put 'im through,' snapped Mr. Budd. There was a moment's delay, and then the voice of Professor Locksley came over the wire.

'Hello. Is that Superintendent Budd?' he asked.

'Speakin',' said Mr. Budd.

'This is Locksley,' went on the Professor. 'A very curious thing has occurred, and I thought you ought to

198

know about it. If it's a coincidence, it's a very strange one. It concerns that — er — girl who called to see me while you were here this morning. Do you remember?'

'I remember,' said Mr. Budd. 'I passed her in the hall as I went out . . . '

'Miss Karina, she called herself,' said Locksley. 'She is, so she told me, an Egyptian. She had heard that I was engaged in writing a history of ancient Egypt and she came to offer me certain information that she thought I should find useful. There is not the slightest doubt that she is thoroughly conversant with the subject. Some of the things she told me were quite unknown to me before, and she offered explanations for others that have puzzled both myself and my fellow Egyptologists for years. She said she came from a very old family that dated back for centuries and could be traced to a line of priests in the reign of Amen the Third. It sounded incredible, but she assured me that she had records that vouched for the truth of her statements. But it wasn't this that caused me to ring you up. It was the fact that during the course of our conversation she mentioned the Seven Lamps.'

'Oh, she did, did she?' murmured Mr. Budd. 'Now that's very interestin', very interestin' an' peculiar.'

'I thought so, too,' said Locksley. 'She asked me if I was aware if they had ever been found. I told her that I was not, and that as far as I knew there was nothing to prove that they ever existed.'

'What did she say to that?' asked Mr. Budd.

'She disagreed with me,' answered Locksley. 'She said that the story of the Lamps had been handed down in her family from generation to generation. To say that I was astonished would be to put it mildly. I was utterly amazed. Apart from the manuscript translation of the papyrus in my possession, I had never heard any reference to these Lamps of the Gods. I began to get very interested in this woman who called herself Miss Karina. It would be a great discovery on my part if I could really prove that the Lamps existed. I questioned her closely about them, and she certainly knew all there was to be known — and more. She said that they had been removed from their original resting place, and lost, and she had wondered whether I, who was well known as an authority on such things, had any knowledge of their present whereabouts. It became quite evident to me that her real reason for coming was to pump me regarding the Lamps. Now, what do you make of it?'

'Nuthin',' said Budd. 'But it's worth followin' up, all the same. Where can I get hold of 'er?'

'She gave me an address in Wimbledon,' replied Locksley. 'I have it here. The Old House . . . '

The big man found a pencil and wrote it down.

'Do you think she was tellin' the truth — about comin' from a line of priests?' he asked, and there was an appreciable pause before the other replied.

'I should hesitate to pass an opinion on that,' he said at length. 'I can only tell you that she was very definitely of Egyptian origin.'

'She never mentioned Karolides?' asked Mr. Budd.

'No,' said Professor Locksley, 'she never mentioned Karolides.'

'Well, I'm very much obliged to you, sir,' said Mr. Budd. 'What you've told me is very interestin', an' I'll certainly look into it.'

'I'll be glad if you will let me know what you find out,' requested Locksley. 'I'm very interested.'

Mr. Budd promised and rang off. For several seconds he sat staring at the desk before him, his lips pursed and his brows drawn together. Here was a fresh development that might mean a lot, or nothing. It would be very strange if this mention of the Seven Lamps by Professor Locksley's visitor was only a coincidence; almost too strange to believe in. And if it wasn't a coincidence, then she must know something. But the Seven Lamps that she talked about were *not* the seven lamps connected with Karolides — that is, not if the lamp found in Lew Glomm's room was a specimen. Yet surely there could not be *two* sets of lamps . . . ? Mr. Budd scratched his head. It was certainly a teaser. He got up, put on his hat and coat, and left the office. Perhaps if he had a word or two with this woman who called herself Miss Karina, he might learn something further? It was worth a visit to Wimbledon to find out . . .

3

He had no difficulty in locating The Old House. It was, apparently, a well-known landmark in the district, and the first person he asked was able to direct him. He drove slowly up the drive and brought his shabby little car to a halt in front of the porch. In answer to his ring, the door was opened by an Egyptian servant in native costume, who stared at him questioningly.

'Does Miss Karina live here?' asked Mr. Budd. The man bowed. 'I should like to see her for a few minutes,' the big man continued. 'Give 'er my card, will you?' He held it out and the servant took it and departed.

Mr. Budd surveyed the unusual furnishings of the hall with sleepy-eyed interest. Although he knew very little about such things, he could tell that the objects around him were of priceless value. There was money here, a lot of money.

After the lapse of perhaps a minute, the Egyptian servant came back. With a low bow he indicated that Mr. Budd was to follow him, and led the way through a curtained archway to a door, which he opened and then stood aside. Mr. Budd found himself in the big, black, green and gold room where Karina and the old man had waited for the coming of Khyfami on the night of Karolides' death. Karina, dressed now in a conventional suit of soft black material, which fitted her lovely figure like a glove, was standing before the golden settee, his card in her hand. Except that she no longer wore her hat and furs, she was dressed as he had seen her earlier that day at Professor Locksley's house. She recognised him. He saw the look of recognition come into her almond-shaped eyes.

'You wished to see me?' she said, with only the very slightest trace of an accent.

'Yes, Miss,' answered Mr. Budd. 'I want to ask you a few questions concernin' a matter which I'm investigatin' . . . '

'Questions?' she said, and frowned slightly. 'Didn't I see . . . weren't you at

Professor Locksley's this morning?'

'That's right, Miss,' replied the big man. 'I was just leavin' when you arrived . . . '

'And you want to ask me questions?' she said, looking a little puzzled. 'What kind of questions? What about . . . ?'

Mr. Budd cleared his throat.

'On the night of November the Eighth,' he said, slowly, 'a man was killed in an empty house in Court Road, Berrydale. He was murdered. His name was Arturus Karolides. Can you give me any information concernin' him?'

'Why should you think I can?' she asked.

'I 'ave several reasons for thinkin' you can,' answered Mr. Budd. 'Would you mind givin' me a straight answer to my question?'

Before she could reply the door opened and a man came quickly into the room Mr. Budd saw that he was tall, dark, and olive-skinned.

'Who is this man, Karina?' he asked, sharply.

'He has come from the police,' said the

girl. She handed him the card and he glanced at it swiftly.

'You are the person whose name is on this?' he said, turning to Mr. Budd, and he nodded. 'What do you want?'

'I've already explained to the young lady,' replied Mr. Budd, patiently. 'I'm investigatin' the murder of a man called Karolides, an' . . . '

'What has it to do with us?' demanded Khyfami. 'We know nothing of how he died.'

'Maybe not,' said the superintendent. 'I 'aven't suggested that you do. All I want ter know is everythin' you can tell me about Karolides . . . '

'How do you know that we knew Karolides?' said Khyfami.

'The p'lice get to hear o' things,' said Mr. Budd, who until that moment had *not* known, but certainly did now. 'It's not usual for us ter give away the source of our information . . . '

'I was acquainted with the man, Karolides,' said Khyfami. 'We had some business dealings together. This lady never met him . . . '

'You 'ad business dealin's with him, did you?' said Mr. Budd. 'Well, that's very interestin'. Would they be connected with the Seven Lamps, by any chance?'

The effect of his words was electrical. The girl uttered a small, quick little cry that was partly a gasp, and stared at him with wide eyes. Khyfami, his emotions under better control, gave no spectacular display of his startled astonishment, but the change in his face was expressive.

'What,' he said, and his voice was a trifle harsh and rasping, 'do *you* know about the Seven Lamps?'

'Nuthin' very much,' answered Mr. Budd, 'but I'm willin' to learn. In fact, I'm very anxious to learn . . . '

'How did you know anything about them?' demanded Khyfami, but instead of answering the question, Mr. Budd replied with another.

'What had Karolides got to do with 'em?' he asked.

There was an appreciable silence. Khyfami looked quickly at the girl and then back at Mr. Budd. At last he said:

'Sit down — er — Superintendent. I

rather think you and I should have a little talk . . . '

'I rather think so, too,' agreed Mr. Budd. He sat down gingerly on a carved ebony chair that felt more comfortable than it looked. 'Who's goin' ter start?' he said.

'You,' said Khyfami. 'What makes you believe that Karolides had anything to do with the Seven Lamps?'

The stout superintendent told him of the finding of the scrap of paper under the dead man's body.

'So,' said Khyfami, and nodded. He thought for a moment, and then he went on: 'You know what the Seven Lamps are?'

'Professor Locksley read a description of 'em out of an old book,' replied Mr. Budd. 'That's all I know about 'em . . . '

'Professor Locksley, ah!' said Khyfami, and nodded again. 'I understand. This Professor Locksley . . . did he know Karolides?'

'*I* came 'ere to do the questionin',' remarked Mr. Budd, gently.

'You . . . ? Ah, yes, I understand. I will

supply some of the answers,' said Khyfami. 'You ask what information I can give regarding Karolides? A little, but not much. He was what you call an adventurer, a crook, but you knew that already? Knowledge had come to him regarding the whereabouts of the Lamps . . . He offered to sell them to me at a price — a very high price. I paid him part of the money and he made several appointments to give me the Lamps and receive the balance. There were always excuses . . . each time I met him he had a fresh one. There had been a delay in getting them . . . the man who was bringing them had not arrived . . . There had been a difficulty in getting hold of them . . . At last he made a final appointment at his rooms in Cumberland Street. The Lamps were in his possession at last. If I would bring the money, he would hand them over to me . . . I went with the money. He was out and I waited, but he did not come. I waited all the evening, but he did not come. That is all I know of Karolides.'

He had said nothing about his visit to

Berrydale and the finding of Karolides, dead, in the empty house.

'How,' asked Mr. Budd, in his sleepy way, 'did Karolides think he was goin' to get hold of these Lamps?'

Khyfami shook his head.

'That I do not know,' he replied. 'He refused to tell me that. He was connected with many strange people and he had stumbled upon the whereabouts of the lost Lamps by accident . . . '

'The *lost* Lamps?' repeated Mr. Budd, questioningly. 'There was nuthin' about the Lamps bein' lost in that book o' Professor Locksley's. They was s'posed ter be inside some pyramid . . . '

'The Lamps were stolen many thousands of years ago,' said Karina.

'May I ask 'ow you know that, Miss?' inquired the big man, turning toward her.

'It is written in the records of my family,' she answered simply. 'The founder of my family was the High Priest Ra-Harmachis, who was known as the Keeper of the Lamps. We have all been under a cloud of disgrace since they were stolen, and this will not be lifted until they are restored.'

Mr. Budd listened, his mind full of wonderment. This girl was talking about something that had happened thousands of years ago as if it had been yesterday. Surely after all this time it couldn't matter whether the Lamps were restored or not? And yet she seemed to take the whole thing seriously, as if the restoration of the Lamps was something of vital importance. These people looked at things differently, he supposed.

'I see,' he said, slowly, which was not strictly true, because he didn't see at all. 'An' how was it you came in contact with Karolides?'

'For generations Karina's family has been trying to find some trace of the Lamps,' answered Khyfami. 'Throughout the ages they have tried, employing many people in the search, but without success. And then a year ago one of our agents received a hint. It was nothing more. A man had been heard talking to another in a café in Cairo. There was a mention of Seven Lamps . . . It was enough for the matter to be reported to me. The man was traced. He knew nothing. He had

212

only repeated something *he* had heard . . . The trail was followed slowly and laboriously, and eventually led to the Greek, Karolides. The rest I have told you.'

'Are you a member of the family of this High Priest What's-his-Name?' asked Mr. Budd.

'No, no.' Khyfami smiled and shook his head. 'I am only a humble servant of the house . . . '

'An' you really believe that Karolides knew where these Lamps were to be found?'

'I did believe it,' replied Khyfami, simply. 'I still believe that he was in possesson of the secret . . . '

'But you didn't just take his word for it?' said Mr. Budd. 'He produced some kind o' evidence to prove what he claimed?'

'He described the Lamps to me,' said Khyfami, 'and I regarded that as sufficient proof.'

'Well, it wouldn't have satisfied *me*,' declared Mr. Budd. 'Not with a feller like Karolides.'

'How could he describe them unless he had seen them?' replied Khyfami.

'Professor Locksley described 'em to me an' 'e'd never seen 'em,' said the stout superintendent. ''E got 'is description out of a book . . . '

'I cannot understand that,' broke in Karina. 'The only existing account of the Lamps is in our possession . . . '

'You're wrong there, Miss,' said Mr. Budd. 'I've *seen* this book of Professor Locksley's. It's very old an' it's hand-written. 'E said no other copy existed. He said it was the translation of a papyrus . . . '

'You suggest that Karolides obtained his information from this book?' said Khyfami, quickly.

'No, I don't,' Mr. Budd disclaimed. 'Karolides didn't know 'im according to Professor Locksley . . . '

'Then why was he . . . ' Khyfami stopped, realising the danger of what he had been going to say.

'Why was 'e, what?' inquired Mr. Budd, softly.

'Nothing,' said Khyfami. 'I was speaking without thinking.'

Like hell you were, thought the stout superintendent. You were goin' to say: 'Then why was he on his way to see him when he was killed,' or something very like it. And how did you know that? Aloud he said:

'What made you go an' see Professor Locksley today, Miss?'

'He is known as a very famous Egyptologist,' replied Karina. 'His knowledge of ancient Egypt is very profound. I went to see if he knew anything of the Lamps . . .'

'But I understood you ter say, Miss,' murmured Mr. Budd, 'that the only existin' account o' the Lamps was in your possession. Why did you expect that Professor Locksley'd know anything about 'em?'

'I just thought there was a chance that he might,' she said, calmly.

'Karolides was killed in an empty house in the road next to Professor Locksley's road,' said Mr. Budd, suppressing a yawn. 'Did you know that?'

'Not until you told us,' she answered quickly.

'Rather a queer coincidence that he should have been killed almost next door, as yer might say, to Professor Locksley, don't yer think?' said Mr. Budd.

'Very strange indeed,' agreed Khyfami, regarding him steadily. 'Can you account for it?'

'Not yet I can't,' admitted Mr. Budd, candidly.

'It would almost seem,' went on Khyfami, smoothly, 'that Professor Locksley is lying when he says he did not know Karolides . . .'

'Maybe,' said the big man. 'Or maybe it was Karolides who knew Professor Locksley. Did Karolides ever mention a man called Lew Glomm to you?'

Khyfami shook his head.

'Or a place called The Sacred Ibis, run by a feller named Ahmadun?'

Khyfami continued to shake his head.

'Well, it's all very queer,' said Mr. Budd, with a sigh. 'A regular mix-up if ever there was one. Maybe it'll straighten itself out.' He rose to his feet and picked up his hat. 'I'm sorry you can't help more'n you 'ave,' he said, sorrowfully.

'But I'm much obliged for what you 'ave told me. P'raps somethin'll crop up an' you'll be able to 'elp me more.'

'We shall be only too pleased,' murmured Karina, politely.

I'm not so sure of that, thought Mr. Budd, as the Egyptian servant showed him out. It's the things you *haven't* told me that would be the interesting ones. Oh, well, maybe we shall be meeting again soon . . . He got heavily into his dilapidated little car and drove slowly down the neglected drive. As he came to the gate, a man turned in from the roadway and stood aside for the car to pass him. Mr. Budd glanced at him, and then his foot came down sharply on the brake pedal and the car shuddered to a standstill.

'I'd like a word with you,' he said gently, thrusting his head out of the window. It was the man whom Lew Glomm had met at The Sacred Ibis on the previous night.

4

The man, who was still wearing the fawn-coloured raincoat, did not appear in the least disconcerted or alarmed. His pleasant, good-looking face wore a slightly surprised expression as he came forward to the car.

'Sure,' he said. 'What do you want?'

The accent was American. The man hailed from the United States.

'You was in a club last night,' said Mr. Budd. 'A place called The Sacred Ibis . . . '

'I guess that's right,' was the reply. 'What about it?'

Mr. Budd opened the door of the car and clambered out.

'You were with a feller called Lew Glomm,' he said.

The American made no attempt to deny it. With a faintly puzzled expression he regarded Mr. Budd intently.

'Are you a friend of Glomm's?' he asked.

'I'm a police officer,' answered Mr. Budd. 'C.I.D., New Scotland Yard. What's your name?'

The puzzled expression changed to a look that was vaguely alarmed. 'Gary Janson,' he replied. 'Say, what's the idea . . . ?'

'At the moment, that you an' I should 'ave a little talk,' said Mr. Budd. 'Get in the car an' we'll go into Wimbledon an' find a place where we can get a cuppa tea . . . '

'I'm just on my way to visit some friends,' protested Janson.

'You can visit 'em later — maybe,' snapped the superintendent. 'You're comin' with me . . . '

'Say, what *is* this?' demanded the other, angrily. 'You can't push me around . . . '

'That's your mistake,' said Mr. Budd, curtly. 'Come on, get in.'

'I'll see you in hell . . . ' began Janson.

'I'll see you in the nearest cell if you don't do as you're told,' broke in the big man. 'So you'd better come along.'

The other hesitated. Then, with a shrug of his shoulders, he got into the car.

'I guess I don't know what this is all about,' he said, 'but I suppose you do . . . ?'

'You bet I do,' grunted Mr. Budd, and sent the car spinning out into the roadway. While the engine of that ancient machine was running, it was quite impossible to hold any kind of conversation. The noise was terrific. They exchanged no word, therefore, until they arrived at a small teashop in Wimbledon and were seated at a vacant table.

'Now,' said Janson, 'perhaps you'll explain what this means?'

'It's you what's goin' ter do the explainin',' said Mr. Budd. He ordered tea from the waitress who came up and, when the girl had gone, continued: 'There's quite a lot of explainin' fer you to do, Mr. Janson, so you'd better get ready to talk, an' talk fast . . . '

'I guess I don't like your attitude, Mr . . . ?'

'Budd,' supplied the big man. 'Sup'ntendent Robert Budd, C.I.D., New Scotland Yard. An' so far as my attitude is concerned, I'm bein' pretty good. I'm givin' yer tea, instead of takin' you to the nearest police station . . . '

'But what's the big idea?' demanded Gary Janson. 'What am I supposed to have done?'

'That's what I 'ope this little talk's goin' ter clear up,' said Mr. Budd. 'Why did you meet Lew Glomm at The Sacred Ibis last night?'

'Well, I don't see that that's anybody's business but his and mine,' said the American. 'This is a free country, isn't it?'

'Up to a point,' retorted Mr. Budd. 'There are certain things that ain't allowed, an' murder's one of 'em . . . '

'Murder?' Janson stared at him.

'Lew Glomm was murdered in his lodgin's in Lamb Street last night,' said Mr. Budd, and watched under his lowered lids to see what effect this sudden statement would have on the man opposite him. It produced nothing but complete bewilderment mingled with a trace of horror.

'Gee, that's terrible!' he exclaimed. 'How did it happen?'

'That's what I want *you* to tell *me*,'

answered Mr. Budd. 'You met Lew at the Ibis an' you left with him. I was there an' I saw you. So far as is known, *you* were the last person to see 'im alive . . . '

'Say,' cried Janson, leaning forward quickly. 'You don't think I . . . '

'Your description has been circulated to all stations an' patrols with instructions ter pull you in on sight,' said Mr. Budd. 'That's why I said you was lucky to be sittin' 'ere having tea with me. If you'd run into an ordinary p'liceman you'd 'ave been lugged off to the cooler . . . '

'But I have nothing to do with it,' declared Janson. 'Why, I left Glomm just outside that place. He was well enough then.'

'Can you prove that?' demanded Mr. Budd, and the other was silent. 'I see you can't. It's only your bare word, an' I'm afraid it ain't goin' very far. You was the last person with Glomm . . . '

'But I never went near his lodgings,' protested Janson. 'He said he had an appointment . . . '

'He 'ad, with me,' interrupted Mr. Budd. 'An' when I kept it, I found 'im dead. There's nothin' to show that you didn't go home with him. There was nobody else in the house except 'is landlady, and she was so drunk you could 'ave blown up the street an' she wouldn't have known it.'

'I guess it looks as though I'm in a spot,' said Gary Janson, quietly.

'You are,' agreed Mr. Budd, candidly. 'The best thing I can suggest you do is ter come clean . . . '

'I'm not going to confess I killed Glomm, when I didn't,' said the American. 'You can third degree me as much as you like . . . '

'We don't use the third degree in England,' said Mr. Budd.

The waitress brought the tea and he waited until she had left it on the table and gone.

'What I meant by 'comin' clean' was let's 'ave the truth. What did you 'ave ter do with Glomm?'

Gary Janson did not answer at once. He appeared to be considering. Mr. Budd poured out two cups of tea and pushed one across the table.

'It's no good tryin' to hide up things,' he said. 'People 'ave got themselves in more trouble by tryin' to 'ide up things than if they'd come out with the truth at the beginnin'. If you didn't kill Glomm, then you've got nuthin' to fear from me, an' if you did, all the hidin' up in the world won't help you.'

The young American looked at him steadily.

'I didn't kill him,' he said. 'That's all I can tell you.'

'You realise what you're lettin' yourself in for?' said Mr. Budd, warningly. 'It'll be my duty to detain you on suspicion . . . '

Gary Janson's face tightened and he shrugged his shoulders.

'Sure,' he replied. 'I guess I'll just have to take a chance . . . '

5

'He won't talk, sir,' said Mr. Budd, two hours later, to the Assistant Commissioner. ''E just declares that he didn't kill Glomm an' refuses to say anything more.'

Colonel Blair scratched the side of his face irritably.

'I don't see what else you could have done,' he said, 'but I don't like it. There's sure to be trouble. The Embassy'll get in touch with the Foreign Office and there'll be a flood of minutes from Whitehall. Somebody'll start asking questions in the House, and the newspapers will run leading articles . . .'

'I gave 'im every chance to explain, sir,' said Mr. Budd.

'I'm sure you did,' answered the Assistant Commissioner. 'I'm not blaming you, or suggesting that you should have acted any differently. You had to detain him on the evidence, but his father is a big noise in America — a multi-millionaire — and he'll stir up all the trouble he can when he hears about it. Oh, well,' he waved his hand impatiently, 'it can't be helped. We'll just have to sit tight and bear the brickbats as well as we can. You think he's guilty?'

'Well, sir,' answered the big man, cautiously, 'the evidence points that way, but I wouldn't like to say I was sure of it. If he killed Glomm, then 'e killed Karolides as well. I'm pretty sure the same person was responsible for both crimes.'

'I think you're right,' agreed Colonel Blair. 'It's a queer business altogether. If we could only find out what's at the back of it. There was the attack on the girl, too. Do you believe this fellow Janson was responsible for that as well?'

'It follows naturally, doesn't it, sir?' said Mr. Budd. 'Miss Hartley saw something in that empty house which she can't remember, an' it's my opinion that the attempt on her life was in case she should. There's nothin' else, that I can see, that connects 'er with the business at all.'

'How could he know about that?' said the Assistant Commissioner, frowning. 'How could he know that this girl had seen something that she couldn't remember?'

Mr. Budd shook his head.

'That's a bit puzzlin', I'll admit,' he said. 'She mentioned it to Professor Locksley an' to his nephew, an' to her employer, Mr. Tape. Maybe she talked to other people. It's surprisin' 'ow things get around sometimes . . . '

'It's all very complicated,' said Colonel Blair. 'What about these people at Wimbledon and the Seven Lamps? That sounds like something out of the Arabian Nights . . . You found a lamp hidden in Glomm's room, didn't you?'

'Yes, sir, but it doesn't help,' replied Mr. Budd. 'I took it to Professor Locksley an' 'e says that it's of no value at all — not more'n a few pounds, anyway . . . '

'Locksley?' remarked the Assistant Commissioner, musingly. 'He's a pretty big man in his own sphere. It seems incredible to suppose that he could be mixed up in anything like this, but . . . '

'I 'aven't failed to take it into consideration, all the same, sir,' said Mr. Budd, 'and I'm checkin' up on him . . . '

'I think you're wise,' agreed Colonel Blair. 'And there's Ahmadun, too. Something must have prompted him to plan that attack on you. He must have been afraid of what you knew, or what you might find out, and it wouldn't be in connection with that club of his. The police have been wise to that for a long time . . . ' He sighed and leaned back in his chair. 'There's such a devil of a lot of loose threads about this business,' he complained. 'You can see the end of 'em, but they don't lead anywhere. Why was this fellow Karolides going to see Professor Locksley that night? What game was he playing with those people at Wimbledon? What connection had Glomm with it and with him? Why the deuce did he hide a lamp that is of practically no value? What business could this man Janson, the son of an American multi-millionaire, possibly have with a crook like Glomm — business which he'd sooner risk a charge of murder than disclose? It's nothing but a series of questions without answers.'

Mr. Budd listened a little wearily. He had asked himself these same questions over and over again.

'It's my experience, sir,' he said, suppressing a yawn, 'that in a case like this, you've got ter find the key question an' the right answer. All the rest sort of pop up automatically then an' answer themselves . . . '

'That's right as far as it goes,' said Colonel Blair. 'But which is the key question here? Who killed Karolides, I suppose?'

Very slowly, Mr. Budd shook his head.

'No, sir,' he answered. '*I* wouldn't call that the key question. I'd say, what was the reason that took Karolides to Berrydale? I'd say *that* was the key question, sir.'

The Assistant Commissioner considered this for a while in silence, and then he nodded.

'Yes, I think perhaps you would be right,' he said. 'When is the inquest on Karolides?'

'In the mornin' at ten o'clock,' answered Mr. Budd. 'There won't be much to it. Evidence of identification an' the medical evidence, that's all, sir. I've seen the Coroner an' he's willin' to agree to an adjournment. I'm goin' ter see these people at Wimbledon tonight. When I found Janson he was on his way to the 'ouse. I'm goin' to see what they can tell me about him.'

'That's quite a good idea,' said Colonel Blair. 'And do see if you can make that young idiot talk. If he didn't kill Glomm it might save us all a lot of trouble.'

'I'll do me best, sir,' said Mr. Budd, and left the office.

* * *

Whatever hopes Jill Hartley may have had that her snubbing of Richard Wayland would have the effect of damping that gentleman's ardour were destroyed when she answered the telephone and heard his cheerful voice greet her over the wire.

'Hello, Jill,' he said. 'What are you doing this evening? Would . . . '

'I'm going to the pictures, and then I'm going home,' she replied, coldly. 'I told you *not* to ring me up, Mr. Wayland . . . '

'I'm very fond of the movies,' he remarked, ignoring her rebuke. 'Why not let me take you . . . ?'

'Because I prefer to go alone,' she broke in quickly.

'You *are* an unsociable girl,' he said. 'I'll come and meet you outside the office . . . '

'If you do,' she snapped, 'you'll get a shock. I am being guarded by a detective from Scotland Yard, who follows me wherever I go. I'm sure that if he thought I was being annoyed he'd . . . '

'You *do* go to a lot of trouble to keep off your admirers, don't you?' he said, and she felt herself redden.

'You know very well he is not there for that reason,' she exclaimed, angrily. 'I think you're insufferable, Mr. Wayland!' She banged the telephone down on its hook before he could reply.

Richard Wayland chuckled. For a moment he thought of recalling her, and then decided that he would leave it.

Leaving the instrument he strolled, whistling softly, into the drawing room and stood at the big windows staring out. His Uncle was busy in his study and had threatened dire penalties for anyone who disturbed him. Mrs. Moule had been called away suddenly to visit a sick sister, and the girl who came in daily to help was valiantly trying to cope with everything in her absence, with the result that the lunch had been late and almost uneatable, and the prospect of tea was problematical. Richard Wayland was feeling a little fed-up and more than a little bored. He exhausted the scanty attractions of the view from the window and, turning back into the room, began to move about in a restless, desultory manner, picking up a book here and straightening an ornament there, in the way people do when they are at a loose end and can't make up their minds what to do next.

He was a trifle irritated that he could make no headway in his relations with Jill. He found her far more attractive than any of the girls he had previously known, but she would have nothing to do with him. The breezy methods, which he had always found successful before, had no effect with her at all. And the more she snubbed him, the more determined he became to break down the barriers she put up. If constant dripping would wear away a stone, it ought to have some result with a girl, he thought. Persistence usually won in the long run with anything. Perhaps it would be a good idea to see her in person. There was plenty of time to reach Mr. Tape's office before she left . . . It would be something to do, anyhow. Anything was better than rambling about the house like this . . .

He put on his hat and coat and went out. When he got to the station he found that a train for Waterloo had just gone, and there would not be another for half an hour. He nearly decided to give it up and go back to the house, but the prospect of spending the rest of the afternoon loafing about seemed so depressing that he elected to carry out his original project. Even the station was preferable. He hung about, pacing the platform and smoking innumerable cigarettes, until the train came in.

It was half-past five when he reached Waterloo, and hailing a taxi he was driven to the offices of Messrs. Tape, Redman and Tape. As he dismissed the cab he noticed, idly, that a large and expensive-looking private car was drawn up at the kerb outside the entrance. A man was sitting in the back, and there was a chauffeur at the wheel, but in the gloom it was impossible to see what either of them were like. He concluded that the car belonged, most probably, to one of Mr. Tape's more prosperous clients.

He lit a cigarette and walked slowly past. It was a dry, cold evening, and there were signs that the night would bring with it a stiff frost. Richard walked to the corner of the street, turned, and came leisurely back again. He wouldn't have long to wait before Jill came out. It was already ten minutes to six, and she usually left punctually. He wondered what sort of reception he would get. She would be annoyed, possibly *very* annoyed, he thought ruefully, but it would be worth it.

It would prove to her that all the snubbing in the world wasn't going to put him off. Supposing she did call the detective . . . ? By the way, *where* was the detective? There appeared to be nobody else, but himself loitering about. He looked up and down the street, but he could see no sign of anyone that looked like a detective. There was a youth with a large bundle of letters, which he was obviously going to put in the pillar-box nearby, and a girl with an attaché-case, evidently on her way home, but there was nobody else. He became so intent in trying to discover the illusive detective that he very nearly missed Jill as she came hurrying out. As it was he was only just in time to see her cross the pavement and step into the waiting car. Before he had time to recover from his surprise, it had driven off . . .

6

Jill had been in sole charge of the office that afternoon. Mr. Tape had not come back after lunch, having an appointment at the house of an important client who was paralysed and could not come to the office. This was a periodical affair which happened on an average every six weeks, when the old lady in question decided to alter her will. Mr. Tape was never very enthusiastic about it, but it was a large estate involving a considerable sum of money and a very large amount of property and, since his firm had acted for the family for many generations, there wasn't very much he could do about it. It was almost immediately after she had hung up on Richard Wayland that the telephone rang again. She thought that it was Richard Wayland again, and was prepared with a caustic reply, when quite a different voice came over the wire. It was a soft, polite voice; she imagined that it must belong to an upper servant from its deferential quality. Would Miss Hartley very kindly join Mr. Tape at the house of his client immediately she left the office? Mr. Tape required her to take down certain instructions that were rather voluminous. A car would be sent to wait for her at a few minutes before six.

Jill said 'All right,' and rang off with a sigh. Her evening at the pictures would have to be postponed, and she had been looking forward to seeing a particular film. Oh well, she could go on the following evening. It didn't really make so very much difference, except that she hated to have her arrangements upset. It was unusual for Mr. Tape to send for her after business hours. He was a great believer in keeping strictly to time. The office closed at six, and at six precisely everybody packed up and went home, neither a minute before nor a minute after. She supposed that this was in the nature of an emergency. Perhaps the old lady was being unusually difficult about the disposal of her property.

She settled down to her work and put

the matter out of her mind until it was time to go. At five minutes to six she put the cover on her typewriter, locked the papers she had been working on in a drawer, and tidied herself up. She saw the car as she came down the stairs, and the chauffeur got out and opened the door. Her foot was on the running board, and she was half inside, before she saw that there was someone sitting in a corner of the back seat . . .

'Please get in, Miss Hartley,' said the voice that had spoken over the telephone. 'I have been instructed to accompany you . . .'

The slight accent seemed more marked, and for the first time a sudden misgiving assailed her. She hesitated, and a hand reached out, caught her arm, and pulled her into the car. A cloud of something that smelled like incense puffed into her face, and she gave a quick, involuntary gasp. The spice-like powder filled her lungs and her nostrils. A languor that was infinitely soothing and restful enveloped her, permeating her whole being. The car, the man in the corner, the cold, frosty November night faded. She was floating in warmth and sunlight down a delightful stream that flowed on and on, placidly, for all eternity . . .

'Drive on,' ordered Khyfami, and, as the car slid softly forward, he gently settled the unconscious girl in the corner . . .

★ ★ ★

Jill began to dream. She dreamt that she was lying on a soft divan in a room that was like no other room she had ever seen. The walls and ceilings were draped with silken hangings of a delicate shade of purple. It was a lovely purple that seemed to glow with a light of its own, entirely independent of the lamp which hung on slender silver chains from the centre of the room. The floor was inlaid with a pale-coloured wood that looked like dull silver, on which were two beautiful rugs of such a fine texture that they gleamed in the soft light. The divan was heaped with cushions of silver and mauve, and beside it was a low table of the same strange wood as the floor, exquisitely carved and bearing a silver tray on which was set a coffee service of black, eggshell thin china. There was no window to this extraordinary dream room and no door. A subtle and rather pleasant perfume filled the air; aromatic and faintly exotic. She felt, as she breathed it, a pleasurable tingling course through her; a tingling that was however, not stimulating, but made her take a sensuous delight in completely relaxing. She lay for some time in this rapturous state, hoping that she would not wake and destroy the illusion, for she was convinced that she was dreaming. None of this could be real — the room, the perfume, the soft divan . . . It was all a dream, but a very pleasant dream. She had no desire to wake and find herself in her own bed in the flat . . . She closed her eyes, and when she opened them again a very old man was standing by the divan, looking down at her. He was dressed in an embroidered robe, and his hair was as white as freshly fallen snow.

'You are awake, O my daughter?' he said, in a thin, gentle voice. 'You have had many dreams, but now you are awake . . . '

'Yes, I am awake,' she answered.

'It is my desire that you will talk with me a little,' said the old man. 'You are at rest, and a great and infinite peace flows through you. You are happy and unafraid.'

'I am happy and unafraid,' she repeated. This was really one of the strangest dreams she had ever experienced, she thought. So vivid and so real, and yet divorced from reality . . . That sounded stupid, and yet it described how she felt.

'That is good,' went on the old man. 'You shall tell me of the man Karolides and of the Seven Lamps . . . '

'I know nothing of Karolides, or of the Lamps,' she said.

'You came to the house where death had taken him,' said the old man. 'You came twice, once alone and again with the police. If you knew nothing of Karolides, what brought you to that house the first time?'

She told him simply and clearly. She could have told nothing but the truth, even if she had wished to do otherwise.

Her brain, from the point of view of thinking coherently in order to work out a lie, was useless . . .

He listened in silence, and his lined face was expressionless. When she had finished, he sighed gently.

'I am assured of the truth of what you tell me, O my daughter,' he said, 'for in your present state you speak with the soul, and the soul cannot be other than truthful. Rest. Bathe in the light that emanates from Ra, which is all-powerful . . . '

He stretched out a skinny hand and chanted something in a tongue that was strange to her. She felt light, with an exquisite sense of joy and freedom such as she had never experienced before. The strange purple room shimmered and appeared to dissolve. Great billows of warmth and radiance flooded over her, and a golden glow swept away the figure of the old man; a golden glow that grew brighter and brighter until it dazzled her eyes and forced her to close them . . .

Harmachis stood watching her for a moment and then, as she began to breathe deeper and more regularly, he moved quietly to one of the walls, lifted a portion of the purple hangings, disclosing a door, and passed softly out. In the big green, black and gold room below, Karina and Khyfami were awaiting him.

'Well?' said the girl, questioningly. 'What have you learned, O my father?'

The old man seated himself on an ebony chair and sadly shook his head.

'She knows nothing,' he answered. He repeated what Jill had told him. 'You see?' he concluded. 'She has no knowledge of that which we seek. Under the influence of the Dust of Truth she was unable to speak falsely . . . '

'I'm beginning to think that we have been following a chimera,' said Khyfami. 'I believe that Karolides was deceiving me about the Lamps. That he had no more knowledge of them than this girl . . . '

'But he described them,' said Harmachis. 'How could he have described them if he had never seen them? The Silver Lamp, the Golden Lamp, the Bronze Lamp . . . ?'

'I know not, O my father,' said

Khyfami, 'but he was a man of evil mind . . .'

'We must not give up hope,' said the girl. 'Perhaps . . .'

She stopped quickly as the door opened and the Egyptian servant appeared on the threshold. He bowed and then began to move his fingers and hands and make gestures in the language of the dumb.

'Shut the door,' ordered Khyfami sharply, and the man obeyed.

'This man is here again,' he said. 'The fat man with the sleepy eyes. What shall we do?'

'We must see him,' said the girl. 'It would look bad if we refused . . .'

'Do you think he has come about the girl?' asked Khyfami.

'How could he know about her?' answered Karina. 'She cannot have been missed . . .'

'Then what brings him here?' he asked. 'Why has he come again so soon . . . ?'

'Let him explain that for himself,' said Harmachis. 'Admit him.'

The servant turned to open the door, but Khyfami stopped him.

'Supposing he *does* know the girl is here?' he said. 'What shall we do?'

'We have not harmed her,' replied the old man. 'Not a hair of her head has been hurt. He can do nothing to us . . . '

'I think you worry without cause, Khyfami,' said Karina. 'He cannot possibly know that the girl is here. It is some other reason that has brought him.' She nodded to the servant. 'Show him in,' she said.

The man departed, and almost immediately returned to usher in Mr. Budd.

'I'm sorry to bother you again,' said the stout superintendent, apologetically. 'But it's somethin' rather important . . . '

'Be seated,' said Harmachis imperiously, and waved a thin hand toward an ebony chair.

'Thank you, sir,' said Mr. Budd, wondering who this venerable old gentleman could be. He waited in the hope that somebody would tell him, but they didn't. 'I've come to ask yer for some information concernin' a man I met at your gate when I was leaving here this mornin' . . . '

'A man at the gate?' repeated the old

man. 'What should we know of a man at the gate?'

'Well, 'e was comin' to see you, so I s'pose he knows you,' said Mr. Budd. 'He said you was friends of his. He's detained at the moment on suspicion o' being concerned in the murder of Karolides and Lew Glomm . . . '

'He was deceiving you if he said that we were his friends,' broke in Harmachis. 'We do not know anyone in this country.'

'He's an American,' said Mr. Budd. 'His name's Gary Janson . . . Look after the young lady!'

Karina gave a little cry and collapsed limply on to the golden settee.

PART FIVE

THE BLOOD OF RAMESES

1

Karina recovered quite quickly. Khyfami hurried to pour out a glass of water from a carafe on a side table, but before he could bring it back to her she was sitting up. She drank some of the water and apologised in a faint voice for her silliness.

'I ought ter be the one to apologise,' said Mr. Budd, shaking his head. 'It was my fault. I shouldn't 'ave sprung it on yer so sudden. You know this man, Gary Janson?'

'We met him in Cairo,' said Khyfami. 'A very pleasant young man . . . '

'A very obstinate young man,' amended Mr. Budd. 'I take it you was quite good friends?'

'We saw quite a lot of him, then,' said Karina. She was leaning back against the cushions and her face was very pale. 'But we know very little about him . . . '

''E's the son of Janson, the American millionaire,' said Mr. Budd. 'How he got mixed up in this business I don't know, but he's in it up to his neck . . . '

'He can't possibly have had anything to do with the murder,' whispered the girl. 'It's impossible . . . '

'Well, I don't know,' remarked the big man. ''E's behavin' very queerly if he's an innocent man . . . '

'In what way?' inquired Khyfami, and Mr. Budd sketched the situation briefly.

'If he'd explain what 'is business was with Glomm,' he said, 'we might get somewhere, but he won't. He just won't talk at all. It's a very stupid attitude to take up. I was wondering, you bein' friends of his, if you couldn't give him a hint as to 'ow stupid he's bein' . . . '

'I don't think he would take very much notice of anything we could say,' said Khyfami, doubtfully.

'You see, we only met him for a while, while in Cairo . . . '

'When I found 'im, he was comin' here,' interrupted Mr. Budd. 'Which shows he 'adn't forgotten you. Maybe, if you saw him an' 'ad a little talk, 'e'd listen to reason . . . '

'Where is he?' asked Karina.

'In Cannon Row police station; that's practically part o' Scotland Yard,' answered the superintendent. 'He hasn't been charged with anythin' yet. We're just detainin' him on suspicion at present, but we'll have to make a definite charge against 'im soon . . .'

'I'll see him,' said the girl, suddenly. 'If you will tell me when I can do so . . .'

'I'll make all arrangements,' said Mr. Budd. 'What about termorrow mornin' at half-past ten? Would that suit you, Miss?'

She nodded.

'Then I'll come along an' fetch you,' he continued. 'In the meanwhile, I'd be glad if you would tell me how you came to meet Mr. Janson?'

'He was staying at Shepherd's Hotel in Cairo when we were there,' said the girl. 'It was the first time he had been to Egypt. He was on a holiday, and we offered to show him the places of interest.'

'I see,' murmured Mr. Budd. 'Just a holiday acquaintance, as you might say?'

'Yes, that's what you would call it, I suppose,' she agreed.

I don't know that I should, thought Mr.

Budd. I'll bet there was a good bit more to it than that. Aloud he said:

'How long ago was this, Miss?'

'The summer before last,' she answered. 'He left before we did, to go back to America . . .'

'Well,' said Mr. Budd, getting ponderously to his feet. 'I won't bother you any more for the present. I'm much obliged to you for what you've told me, although I'm a bit disappointed it isn't more. I'll be callin' fer you at half-past ten in the mornin', Miss.'

'I'll be ready,' said Karina.

Khyfami took Mr. Budd out into the hall.

'Do you believe that this American is responsible for the murders?' he asked, in a low voice.

'Well,' answered the big man, cautiously, 'the evidence is pretty bad against 'im. I wouldn't go so far as to say that it was conclusive . . .'

'What is your personal opinion?' interrupted the other.

'I don't think he actually killed them fellers,' said Mr. Budd, 'but I'm quite sure 'e knows a lot about it.'

Khyfami watched him as he got into his little car and drove off. For some little while after the tail light had disappeared he stood staring into the darkness of the drive, and then, with a sigh, he turned, closed the big door, and went back to the room where the other two were.

Karina was lying back on the golden settee smoking a cigarette, and Harmachis sat in his usual immobile position on the carved ebony chair.

'Why did you promise to see this man Janson?' asked Khyfami, looking at the girl.

'I thought I might help him,' she said.

'But what can you do?' he replied. 'What can you say to him? I think you were unwise . . . '

'It is written,' said Harmachis, in his thin voice, 'that they should meet again. What is written cannot be avoided . . . '

'He was in Berrydale on the night of Karolides' death,' said Khyfami, thoughtfully. 'He was in the very road where it happened. I told you I saw him . . . '

'That does not make him guilty,' said

the girl. 'You, Khyfami, were in the very house, but you did not kill Karolides.'

'No, that is true,' agreed Khyfami. 'But Janson was also with this Glomm man, and he, too, died . . . '

'I do not believe that he would kill any man,' said Karina.

'Then why does he keep silent?' demanded Khyfami.

'There may be other reasons,' she said. 'I will try and persuade him to speak, if he will listen to me . . . '

'I still think it is unwise of you to go,' said Khyfami. 'I must see about getting the girl back to her home . . . '

'How are you going to do that?' asked Harmachis. 'She will be in a dazed condition for several hours. You cannot take her to where she lives, or you may be seen . . . '

'I have thought of that, O my father,' said Khyfami. 'I shall drive her to the railway station at Waterloo and leave her in the waiting room. She will be quite safe there, and when she fully recovers she will be able to make her own way to her home. She will remember nothing of what

254

has happened to her.'

'It is well,' said the old man. 'You had better see to it at once, Khyfami. It was a waste of time bringing her here, for she is ignorant of what we seek . . . '

At four o'clock in the morning Jill woke to find herself, to her intense astonishment, propped up in the corner of an uncomfortable leather seat in the Ladies' Waiting Room at Waterloo Station. She had no recollection of how she had got there, and could remember nothing after she had left Mr. Tape's office and got into the big car which had been waiting. From then until now her mind was a blank. The only recollection she had at all was of warmth and sunshine . . .

When she got back to her flat she looked at herself in the long mirror in the bathroom. There was a bloom on her skin as though she had just come back from a long holiday by the sea . . .

2

The officer unlocked the door of the cell, and Mr. Budd entered with Karina.

'Here's a visitor for yer, Mr. Janson,' he said, and the young man who was seated on the pallet bed looked up. He uttered a quick, startled exclamation as he saw the girl.

'Karina!' he cried.

'I'll leave you two together,' said Mr. Budd genially, and left the cell, closing the door behind him. The next one to it was empty, and into this he slipped quickly. A small, oblong, black box, to which a pair of earphones were attached, rested on the pallet bed, and he put them on. Pressing down a switch on the black box, he listened. The concealed microphone in the adjoining cell picked up all that was being said . . .

'Why did you come here, Karina?' asked the voice of Gary Janson. 'How did you know I was here . . . ?'

'The stout man told me last night,' replied the voice of Karina. 'It is a long time since we last met, Gary. You promised, when you went away to America, that you would write, but you never did . . . '

'I was coming to see you when they detained me,' said Janson. 'You remember giving me your address . . . ?'

'I remember many things, Gary,' said Karina, softly. 'But I thought you had forgotten . . . '

'I didn't forget, Karina,' he said. 'How could I forget? All that I said in Cairo I meant. You believe that?'

'You promised to write, but you didn't,' she said. 'How can I believe anything else you said?'

'There were reasons why I didn't write,' he answered. 'I guess you'll have to take my word for that. I can't tell you what they are . . . '

'Something you found when you got back to America?' she asked.

'Yes, something I found,' he said. 'It's good to see you again, Karina. I guess I just can't tell you how much I've missed you . . . '

'I've missed you, too, Gary,' she said. 'At first it was terrible . . . '

'You must have thought I was a heel,' he said.

'A heel?' she repeated, doubtfully.

'A rotter, a waster,' he explained. 'But I really couldn't help it. I guess you've got to believe that, Karina. I just couldn't help it . . . '

'What happened?' she asked.

'I can't tell you,' he answered. 'It was something that gave me a pretty bad shock . . . '

'Something to do with the reason you're here?' she said.

'Partly, but not entirely,' he replied. 'I guess I got into this spot of trouble on my own. It looks like it was going to be a darned serious spot, too,' he added, gloomily.

'Why don't you tell the police how you got into it?' she said. 'You didn't kill anybody, so what have you got to worry about?'

'Sure, I didn't kill anybody,' he answered, 'but it looks bad and I can't explain . . . '

'But why, Gary?' she persisted.

'Because I can't,' he said. 'I can't explain to anybody. I've just got to face up to it, I guess, and hope for the best.'

'But they may convict you!' she cried, anxiously. 'Gary, do you realise . . . ?'

'Its no good, Karina,' he said. 'I can't talk and that's all there is to it . . . '

'How did you get mixed up with Karolides and this other man?' she asked, curiously.

'Forget it,' he answered. 'If I could tell anyone. I'd tell you. How's Khyfami and Mr. Harmachis?'

'They're both very well,' she replied.

'He's a wonderful old man,' he said, enthusiastically. 'Gee, I hope I'm as well as that when I'm his age.'

'You've got a long way to go,' she said. 'Harmachis is ninety-seven . . . '

'You're kidding?' he declared, incredulously.

'No, it is the truth,' she said. 'His father was over a hundred when he died . . . '

'I thought he was a pretty good age, but not as old as that,' he said. 'I guess he's marvellous . . . '

To Mr. Budd's disgust he began to talk about Cairo, the places they had been to, and the things they had done. He listened in for another quarter of an hour and then he took off the headphones, switched off the amplifier, and went to collect Karina.

'You'll come again?' said Gary Janson, when the girl said goodbye. 'Perhaps I'll be out of this place soon . . . '

'That's up to you, young feller,' remarked Mr. Budd. 'You just tell us what you was doing with Lew Glomm, an' maybe you could leave now.'

'I've said all I'm going to say,' said Gary Janson, stubbornly.

'It's no use,' said Karina, as Mr. Budd escorted her out of the building. 'He refuses to explain anything . . . ' She was a little tearful and depressed. Obviously she was worrying about Gary Janson's ultimate fate if he persisted in his silence, and the big man tried to reassure her as much as he could.

'We'll just 'ave to find things out for ourselves,' he said. 'Don't you worry, Miss. If he didn't have anything to do with these murders, no 'arm'll come to him . . . '

He sent her home in a police car, and made his way laboriously to his small office. Leek was waiting for him with the information that Jill Hartley had rung up, and would he call her back at Mr. Tape's office?

'I wonder if she's remembered?' murmured Mr. Budd, and put the call through. But Jill only wished to tell him about the extraordinary adventure of the preceding evening. Mr. Budd listened in puzzled wonderment.

'Now let's get this right, Miss,' he said, when she had finished. 'You got into a car which you thought Mr. Tape had sent for you, an' you don't remember anything else until you woke up at four o'clock this mornin' an' found yourself in the Ladies' Waitin' Room at Waterloo Station. Is that right?'

'Yes, that's right,' she said. 'And Mr. Tape never sent the car at all. I can't understand what can have happened . . . '

'Did you feel all right when you woke up?' he asked.

'I never felt better before in my life,' she declared. 'And I've felt full of energy all day . . . '

'Interestin' an' peculiar,' said Mr. Budd, thoughtfully. 'You can't recollect anything at all of what happened?'

'Nothing whatever,' she said. 'The whole of that period is just a blank.'

'Queer,' said Mr. Budd. 'I wonder what the idea was? I'll look into the matter, Miss.'

He rang off and looked at Leek.

'Who was the feller tailing Miss Hartley at six o'clock yesterday evenin'?' he asked. 'Find 'im and bring 'im 'ere. I want to have a word with him.'

The lean sergeant departed on his errand, and Mr. Budd slumped back in his chair and lit one of his black cigars. Here was a new thing to chew over. What exactly had happened to Jill Hartley, and why? The girl had obviously come to no harm. In fact, she was feeling very well indeed. What had occurred during that blank period from six o'clock to four o'clock? It seemed fairly evident that she had been taken somewhere in a car, but what had caused the blank in her memory? Certainly no ordinary drug. That would have left her feeling queer . . . What, then? Something new . . . ? And who had been responsible? Not the man who had attacked her at the flat, for surely, if it had been he, he would not have let her come back safe and sound. It was all very perplexing. What was the reason for it? Jill Hartley, without knowing anything about it, seemed to have got herself thoroughly mixed up in the business. Or did she know a lot more than she had said? Mr. Budd sighed wearily. He had seldom, if ever, had such an unsatisfactory case . . .

Leek came back with the unfortunate Detective-Constable whose duty it had been to watch the girl on the previous evening, and Mr. Budd, in one of his most unpleasant and sarcastic moods, gave the man a severe gruelling. It was useless his pleading that he had only been absent from his post for a few minutes while he found a lavatory. It didn't save him from the caustic reprimand.

'Durin' that time,' ended Mr. Budd,

'this girl was whisked away in a car. For all you did to prevent it, she might 'ave been killed . . . '

'I'm very sorry, sir,' apologised the detective, humbly.

'And so you ought ter be,' snarled Mr. Budd. 'You say you saw this car before you left? What make was it, an' what was the number?'

'It was a Cadillac, I think, sir,' began the man.

'You *think*,' snapped Mr. Budd. 'Ain't you sure?'

'No, sir.'

'And the number?'

'I . . . I didn't notice, sir.' The unfortunate detective, very red in the face, looked as though he devoutly wished the floor would open and swallow him up.

'You — didn't — notice,' mimicked the big man. 'You — didn't — notice, an' you call yerself a detective. I s'pose if you was on duty in Westminster they could steal the 'Ouses of Parliament, brick by brick, an' you wouldn't notice? Get out of my sight!'

With a heartfelt prayer of thankfulness,

and surprising alacrity, the man obeyed.

'The only way ter get a job done prop'ly these days is ter do it yerself,' said Mr. Budd, crossly.

'That's what I always say,' agreed Leek. 'Yer can't trust nobody ter do nuthin' . . . '

'Except you,' snarled his superior. 'You can be trusted to do nuthin' all the time.'

Leek, who had brightened a little at the beginning of this speech, relapsed once more into his habitual gloom. For a wild moment he had thought Mr. Budd was going to pay him a compliment.

Still ruffled and annoyed, the superintendent took out a bunch of keys, unlocked a drawer in his desk, and brought out the lamp which the sergeant had found under the floor in Lew Glomm's room. Setting it in the middle of his blotting pad, he sat forward and glared at it with such an unusual look of malignant ferocity that Leek was startled.

'What cher lookin' at that thing like that for?' he asked.

'Like what?' demanded Mr. Budd, curtly. 'Can't you keep quiet when I'm tryin' ter do a bit of concentrated thinkin'?'

'Oh, is that what you was doin'?' said the relieved sergeant.

'You wouldn't understand anythin' about *that*,' said Mr. Budd. 'Ordinary thinkin's beyond you, without the concentrated part of it.' He chewed thoughtfully on the remains of his cigar, which had gone out.

'This lamp's got somethin' ter tell us if we could find out 'ow ter make it talk,' he murmured. 'Why did Glomm take the trouble to 'ide it so carefully if it's of no value?'

'Maybe 'e thought it was,' said Leek, but Mr. Budd shook his head.

'He wouldn't have gone to all that trouble unless he'd *known* it was,' he said. 'Now, how could it be valuable?'

'Somethin' inside it?' suggested the sergeant.

'That's the first thing that occurred to me,' muttered the big man. 'But there ain't nuthin' inside of it. I've had the wick out and looked into the oil chamber, an' it's as empty as your head.' He picked up the lamp and shook it. 'No, there's nuthin' hidden inside it. Unless there's some other place you could put it.'

He hitched himself forward on his chair and drew the lamp closer. Leek shambled over in his ungainly way and leaned on the desk, peering at what Mr. Budd was doing. The lamp stood on a delicately carved base of an intricate filigree design that tapered up to a narrow stem where it met the bulk of the lamp itself. Mr. Budd tried to see if this would unscrew, but it resisted all his efforts.

'Seems solid enough,' he grunted.

'Let me 'ave a go,' said Leek. 'Maybe it's only got stuck.' He took the lamp and twisted with all his strength.

'Here, be careful!' exclaimed Mr. Budd. 'You'll smash . . . '

His warning came too late. There was a sharp snapping crack and Leek stood staring stupidly, the base in one hand and the remainder of the lamp in the other.

'Now look what you've done!' cried Mr. Budd, angrily.

'I couldn't help it,' expostulated Leek. 'It came ter pieces in me 'ands . . . '

'You sound like a servant gal who's broken the best vase,' snarled Mr. Budd. 'Here, give the thing ter me . . . ' He seized the two pieces of the lamp from the dismayed sergeant and looked at them. The break was a clean one. The base had snapped off at the narrow part of the stem, and it was hollow. It was not only hollow, but it was stuffed with some white material that looked like cotton wool.

Mr. Budd, suddenly excited at the possibility that he was about to make an important discovery, picked up a penknife from his inkstand and with the smaller blade began to probe gently into the hollow base.

'What are you doin'?' asked Leek, forgetting the enormity of his offence in his interest.

'I think you may have accidentally found somethin',' said Mr. Budd. 'The lower part of this thing is full o' cotton wool . . . ' He began to tease it out bit by bit. It had been very tightly packed, and it took him a long time, but eventually he succeeded in getting most of it out.

'There is something 'ere!' he exclaimed triumphantly. 'Somethin' solid . . . listen!'

He shook the base of the lamp and something rattled.

3

Whatever it was, it was too large to fall out when he turned the base upside down. He tried to catch a glimpse of it by squinting into the narrow, round orifice, but he could see nothing.

'If there's a way of getting it in there, there must be a way of gettin' it out,' he remarked, frowning. 'Now, let's see . . . ' He made a close inspection of the base, but he could find no means by which whatever was inside had been introduced.

'P'raps it's only a bit of the metal what broke off when the thing was made?' suggested Leek.

'What about all that cotton wool?' grunted Mr. Budd. 'How did that get in there? There must be *some* way . . . ' He tried twisting the base with both hands in the hope that a portion of it would unscrew, but nothing happened.

'Well, I'm going to find out what's inside,' said Mr. Budd. 'An' the only way

that I can see is to break the thing open.
Go an' borrow a hammer and a chisel,
will yer?'

Leek hurried away and was gone for
nearly five minutes. He came back with
the required tools which, he said, he had
had difficulty in getting.

'Where did yer go to get 'em?'
demanded the stout superintendent. 'The
Commissioner's office?'

'No,' answered the sergeant, seriously.
'I didn't know *he* 'ad such things . . . '

'He hasn't,' said Mr. Budd, 'but it's the
sort o' place *you'd* try . . . ' He carried
the base of the lamp over to the fireplace.
'Hold it steady on the hearth,' he said,
and Leek stooped and obeyed. 'Now
don't let go,' continued Mr. Budd, resting
the edge of the chisel on the top of the
round opening. He raised the hammer
and gave a mighty whack. Leek uttered a
yell, and the base of the lamp flew into
the middle of the office.

'What are yer doin'?' cried Mr. Budd,
red in the face from his exertions. 'I
thought I told yer to *hold* it . . . ?'

'That's all very well,' wailed Leek,

looking anxiously at his hand, 'but the chisel slipped an' nearly took the top o' me thumb off . . . '

'Nonsense,' said Mr. Budd. 'It didn't go anywhere near it. Fetch that thing an' let's try again.'

Sucking his injured thumb, Leek shambled over and retrieved the lamp base. Rather unhappily he set it on the hearth, and Mr. Budd prepared to operate once more with the hammer and chisel. This time he succeeded better. The edge of the chisel bit into the soft metal and, after a few blows with the hammer, split it open. Breathing heavily, Mr. Budd picked up the base and, using the chisel as a lever, wrenched it apart. Something fell out and dropped on the floor. Leek made a grab for it.

'Bring it over to the desk an' let's have a look at it,' said the big man, and the sergeant obeyed.

'Looks like a bit o' jewellery,' he remarked. 'Pretty lookin' thing, aint it?'

Mr. Budd took it from him and examined it carefully. It was a large, oval-shaped, red stone, set in dull yellow metal that was finely chased. The stone was clear and of a deep wine colour, and sparkled and scintillated in the light. On each side of the setting was a tiny ring.

'It looks ter me like a ruby,' said Mr. Budd, 'set in gold. An' if it is, it must be worth a good bit. It's nearly as big as a pigeon's egg.'

'No wonder Lew Glomm took such pains to 'ide that lamp,' said Leek. 'I wonder 'ow they got it inside the thing?'

Mr. Budd had a look at the twisted base. Now that it had been ripped open it was possible to see that it was in two parts. The lower half of the base screwed into the upper half. The thread was plainly visible, and the reason why it had failed to unscrew was plainly visible, too, for there were clear traces of corrosion.

'Well, that's how they managed it,' grunted Mr. Budd. He turned his attention once more to the piece of jewellery. 'We'd better get an expert opinion on this right away,' he said, twisting it about in his pudgy fingers. 'I'll take it along to old Aaronson in the Haymarket. He'll know all about it.'

He wrapped it up carefully in a piece of typing paper, and stowed it away in his waistcoat pocket.

'I'll be back soon,' he said, and putting on his hat and coat, left the office.

Mr. Solomon Aaronson occupied a very small office at the extreme top of a very large building. He was a very old man with a bald head and deeply sunken, shrewd eyes, and the greatest expert on precious stones in the world. There was nothing about jewellery that Mr. Aaronson did not know. He could tell you the history of all the famous jewels, where they had been found, who had found them, and their present whereabouts. He had written five thick and lavishly illustrated books on the subject which were regarded as the final word on the matter.

He was sitting at his old-fashioned desk, clad in the velvet jacket, striped trousers and smoking cap that was his habitual attire.

'Good morning, superintendent,' he said, when Mr. Budd was shown in by the elderly clerk. 'It's a long time since you've been here. How are the roses?' He was referring to the big man's hobby.

'They're in very good condition, sir,' said Mr. Budd. 'There's still one or two blooms on the bush roses. They'll be better, I think, next year. I've got a new fertiliser which I'm goin' ter try out, an' from all accounts the results should be very fine.'

Mr. Aaronson removed the short, blackened clay pipe from his lips and smiled.

'Enthusiastic as ever,' he said. 'Well, what can I do for you this time, eh?'

Mr. Budd produced the little packet from his waistcoat pocket and removed the paper.

'I'd like to know what you can tell me about that, sir,' he said, laying the stone in front of the old man.

Mr. Aaronson looked at it, uttered a little sharp ejaculation, and took from a drawer a watchmaker's lens. Screwing it into his right eye, he picked up the jewel delicately in his long, white fingers and carefully examined it.

'How did this come into your possession?' he asked.

Mr. Budd explained.

'Extraordinary,' murmured Mr. Aaronson. 'Extraordinary!' He laid down the jewel, picked up the clay pipe, and tapped the stem against his teeth thoughtfully. Mr. Budd waited as patiently as he could for the information which he knew would be forthcoming. It was useless on these occasions to hurry the old man. He would take his time, but when he *did* speak the superintendent knew that every word he uttered would be unchallengeable.

'This stone is a ruby,' he said at last, 'and is one of seven, equally large and flawless, stones that comprised a necklace known as The Blood of Rameses. It was found during the excavation of a tomb at Karnak in Egypt ten years ago by Professor Phineas Fleming. Mention of it had previously been made in several ancient papyri. It was worn by the reigning King of Egypt and was somewhat the equivalent of our own crown jewels. Many Egyptologists had searched for it without success before Professor Fleming. A great deal of publicity was given to his discovery at the time, for apart from the enormous intrinsic value of the necklace, its historic value was incalculable. Professor Fleming intended presenting it to the museum at Cairo, but his intention was never carried out because the necklace was stolen in transit. The messenger who was carrying it was murdered. From that time, until now, the necklace vanished completely. The Egyptian Government did everything they possibly could to trace it and offered a huge reward for any information concerning its whereabouts. That, briefly, is the history of the necklace of which this jewel once formed a part.'

Mr. Budd listened in increasing wonderment. How had this historic gem come into possession of Lew Glomm?

'You say there were seven rubies, sir?' he asked.

'Yes,' said Mr. Aaronson, 'set in gold like this one and joined together with golden links. You can see the rings where the links were . . . '

'Seven,' murmured Mr. Budd thoughtfully. It was queer, he thought, seven rubies, seven lamps . . . Seven lamps . . . ?

The ruby had been found in a lamp. Did that mean the other six, making the complete necklace, were hidden in lamps, too? Seven rubies, seven lamps . . . This was something more plausible and practical than Professor Locksley's lamps — much more practical. This was something that might have inspired murder . . . He saw Mr. Aaronson looking at him curiously.

'Well, sir,' he said. 'You've given me a lot to think about.'

'When it becomes known that a drop of the Blood of Rameses has been found, it will give quite a lot of people something to think about,' said Mr. Aaronson, quietly. 'You've made a very remarkable and a very sensational discovery, Superintendent. You could almost call it a discovery of international importance. If you could lay your hands on the other six . . . '

'Maybe I will, sir,' said Mr. Budd. 'I suppose I can rely on you to keep this dark for the time bein' . . . ?'

'I think you can,' said Mr. Aaronson.

'You would be surprised at the number of secrets that have never gone beyond these four walls. But be very careful of that . . . ' He nodded at the jewel which lay on his blotting pad like a splash of blood . . . 'I should advise you to lodge it at a bank . . . '

'I'm handin' it over to the Assistant Commissioner,' said Mr. Budd. 'I don't want to have the responsibility of it. Well, I'm very much obliged for your information, Mr. Aaronson. I believe it's goin' ter be of great help . . . '

'I hope so,' said Mr. Aaronson. 'I am always pleased when my knowledge is of help to people. I hope you will let me know if you find the rest of the necklace and, perhaps, let me see it? I should appreciate very much indeed being able to see it. It would be quite an exciting experience, I can assure you.'

Mr. Budd promised that he would do his best and, wrapping up the jewel once more, stowed it away and took his departure.

As he had said, its identification had given him quite a lot to think about. It opened a great number of fresh possibilities. He went back to Whitehall, but instead of entering Scotland Yard he turned into a small teashop. The place was crowded at this hour, but he found a seat at a table and ordered buttered toast and tea. This was his invariable lunch, and, since he was well-known in the place, his order created no astonishment. When his frugal meal was set before him, he ate and drank hungrily and thirstily, and while he munched steadily through his pile of toast he reviewed the case in the light of this fresh discovery . . .

4

Whoever had originally stolen this ancient necklace of the Egyptian kings, it was pretty evident that it had come into the possession of Lew Glomm and Karolides. They might, even, have been responsible for stealing it in the first place. It was just the sort of thing that would have appealed to Karolides. He had dealt mostly in antiques. Mr. Budd considered that it was a great deal more likely, however, that he had bought it from the original thief, for that was the way he had conducted his business. He had had a fairly large clientele among wealthy collectors, who were not too scrupulous about the way they acquired their treasures, and who were willing to pay a good price and no questions asked. He had done a very profitable trade in this way. However he had come into possession of the necklace, it was pretty safe to conclude that its possession was at the root of the murders.

Somewhere there must exist six other lamps, each containing one of the huge rubies of which the original necklace had been composed. Lew Glomm had concealed one: where were the others? And why had Karolides entrusted any of the rubies to Glomm? Lew had not been, by any means, a big man in his profession. He had never risen above being a rather mediocre little burglar. There had never been anything of the specialist about him, like there had with Karolides. That they had been working together, however, was practically certain from the portion of the letter which Leek had discovered in the chimney in Karolides' rooms. There was also a distinct possibility that Mr. Ahmadun was in it, too. It was all very much of a mix-up, thought the big man gloomily. Nothing led anywhere. There was no sequence that could be fitted together. Nothing but a series of facts that were obviously related, but with nothing to show how. What had taken Karolides to Berrydale to see Professor Locksley in such a hurry, and who had been responsible for his death? How had they known he was going in time to prepare the trap which had diverted him to the empty house in Court Road?

The only answer to this seemed to be Locksley himself. If Karolides had notified him that he was coming, he would have been able to set the trap and everything. Could he have been responsible for the murder? There was nothing against such a theory, except the fact that he had been expecting Jill Hartley and would hardly have left the altered road signs for her to find . . . Or would he? Why not? The answer to this was that he would hardly have wished to draw attention to the fact that Karolides had been coming to see him, which was the obvious conclusion for anybody to come to when it was discovered that the names of the roads had been changed. Perhaps in the excitement he had forgotten that Jill Hartley was coming that evening? It seemed scarcely probable that he would, but it was by no means impossible. Supposing he had; what had induced him to kill Karolides? The necklace? But surely if Karolides had been negotiating with him for the Blood of Rameses he would hardly have killed him *before* he had got the necklace in his possession? It was like killing the goose before it had even laid a golden egg . . .

Wait a minute, though, thought Mr. Budd, suddenly. Had he got it, or nearly all of it? Had Karolides brought those other six rubies with him? Perhaps, for some reason, he had been unable to contact Lew Glomm and get the seventh lamp, and had taken the six as a first instalment, as you might say. He would have no suspicion of the possibility of foul play, dealing with a man of Professor Locksley's position and reputation. Mr. Budd came to the conclusion that it was a pretty sound theory, although there were a number of things which it failed to cover. For instance, Gary Janson's connection with the business and his stubborn refusal to talk even to save himself from a murder charge. And that queer group of people at Wimbledon? It did explain, however, why Locksley had tried to sidetrack the significance of the lamps by reading that bit out of the old book . . .

Mr. Budd finished his last slice of toast, poured himself out a third cup of tea, and gulped it down noisily. Wiping his mouth and fingers on his handkerchief, he lit one of his obnoxious cigars, to the scandalised annoyance of the elderly spinster who shared his table, and beckoned his waitress for his bill. He had got a little further, he thought, as he paid the amount at the cashdesk and went out into Whitehall, but not very much. There was nothing clear and well-knit about his theory. It could be knocked to pieces in a dozen ways — Locksley had only to prove that he hadn't left the house that evening to bring it tumbling to the ground. Mr. Budd liked his solutions to be unassailable, and, therefore, he was not satisfied. All the same, it might be useful as a scaffolding on which to erect something more lasting and concrete. More facts were what he wanted . . .

The Assistant Commissioner had just got back from lunch when Mr. Budd sought his interview, and welcomed the big man with unusual geniality.

'Sit down,' he said. 'Well, we've had no

kick from the Foreign Office yet about young Janson, and nobody seems to have raised any questions in the House, but we'll either have to charge him or let him go. We can't keep him detained indefinitely . . . '

'No, sir,' said Mr. Budd. 'There's been a fresh development which I'd like to talk to you about . . . '

'Go ahead,' said Colonel Blair, lighting a cigarette and leaning back comfortably in his chair. Mr. Budd 'went ahead.' He related all that he had done since he had seen the Assistant Commissioner last, and that gentleman punctuated his slow narrative with little nods of approval.

'That was a good idea of yours,' he said, when Mr. Budd reached the point in his story where he had brought Karina to see Janson. 'Pity it didn't lead to a better result.'

'It's my opinion, sir,' said the superintendent, 'that this young feller's screening someone . . . '

'Who?' demanded Colonel Blair.

'I dunno,' said Mr. Budd. 'But that's just how I feel about it. I'm pretty sure he didn't kill either of those two men himself . . . '

'But you think he knows who did?' asked the Assistant Commissioner.

'I wouldn't go so far as that, sir,' said Mr. Budd, shaking his head. 'But I believe 'e knows why they was killed, and it implicates somebody 'e wants to keep out of trouble . . . '

'A woman?' suggested Colonel Blair.

'Well, no, sir. I don't think so,' said Mr. Budd. 'Not after hearin' that girl Karina and him together . . . '

'Why shouldn't it be she?' demanded the Assistant Commissioner. 'In nine cases out of ten, it's a woman when a man won't talk . . . '

'Maybe, sir,' said the superintendent, 'but I think this is the tenth case. Anyhow, I've got somethin' else to tell you. It's really what I came about . . . '

He related to the interested Colonel Blair how he had found the ruby, and the result of his visit to Mr. Aaronson.

'This is really remarkable,' said the Assistant Commissioner when he had finished, examining the jewel which Mr.

Budd had given him. 'This puts quite a different complexion on the case.'

'Yes, sir,' agreed Mr. Budd. 'In some ways it helps, an' in others it don't. It provides a practical an' reasonable motive for the murders . . . '

'But you don't understand, Budd,' interrupted the Assistant Commissioner. 'You don't realise the significance of this in connection with young Janson. I believe that it may explain his refusal to talk.'

'How, sir?' asked Mr. Budd, with sudden interest.

'His father is a well-known collector,' explained Colonel Blair. 'He owns probably the finest collection of pictures, jewellery, and *objects d'art* in the world . . . '

'Is that so, sir?' murmured Mr. Budd. 'Now that's very interestin'.'

'This necklace, the Blood of Rameses, would be just the thing to appeal to him,' went on the Assistant Commissioner. 'Every item in his collection is unique of its kind . . . '

'And you think he would be prepared to purchase these jewels, even though he knew them to be stolen?' said Mr. Budd.

'I should say it was more than likely,' answered Colonel Blair. 'You know what these collectors are. They have a passion for acquiring something that nobody else has got, and in many cases they're not too particular how they come by it. They'd willingly buy it honestly, if it was purchasable, but if not, they're quite willing to get it by other means . . . '

'An' it's your opinion that young Janson was here on behalf of his father to try an' get this necklace from Karolides an' Glomm?' said Mr. Budd.

'Well, it's a suggestion, isn't it?' said the Assistant Commissioner. 'It would account for the fact that he won't say what his business was with Glomm. He couldn't very well explain that he was trying to buy stolen property on behalf of his father, could he?'

'No, I s'pose 'e couldn't,' agreed the big man. 'It also gives him a pretty motive fer killin' these fellers, too, don't it?'

'Yes, it certainly does that,' said Colonel Blair, seriously.

'But it doesn't explain why Karolides

went to see Professor Locksley that night,' went on Mr. Budd, frowning heavily. 'That's the thing that's so puzzling. If we knew that, I think everythin' else 'ud drop into place. I 'ad a kind of vague idea about that . . . ' He told the Assistant Commissioner of his theory concerning Professor Locksley, but Colonel Blair seemed a little dubious in accepting it.

'It doesn't sound very plausible to me,' he remarked. 'I can't imagine a man of Locksley's reputation committing murder. And, in his case, the motive is very weak. This necklace would be of no value to him. He wouldn't want to keep it, and if he wanted to examine it, for the purposes of his book, he would be allowed to do so by applying to the proper authorities — that is, once it was restored, of course. The case of Janson's father is entirely different. His desire is to *possess*, which is common to all collectors. But Locksley only wishes to *discover*. The two mentalities are completely different.'

'There's a certain value to this necklace apart from it's 'istorical one,' said Mr. Budd.

'Yes,' agreed Colonel Blair. 'But that would hardly appeal to Locksley. He's a very rich man, and anyway, he would know that it would be quite impossible to dispose of the thing in an open market. No, I believe you'll be wasting your time if you try to work up a case against Locksley.'

Mr. Budd sighed. He had not been too happy about his theory himself, but it had seemed the only one to account for the way Karolides had met his death.

'Try tackling young Janson with the necklace,' suggested the Assistant Commissioner. 'Tell him that you believe he was trying to buy it from Glomm, and see what he says. Perhaps he'll talk.'

Mr. Budd carried out the suggestion, but without result. Gary Janson listened to all he had to say and maintained a strict and non-committal silence.

5

Mr. Budd spent nearly the whole of the following week in his small and cheerless office frowning over a mass of documents and reports. A full account of the original discovery, and subsequent theft, of the Blood of Rameses had been sent for, and this he carefully and industriously perused, making such notes as he thought would be helpful. There were not many. The messenger, carrying the necklace, had been killed with a knife, and robbed, in the bedroom of an obscure hotel in Cairo. He had arrived at the hotel only an hour before, so it was evident that the murderer must have been keeping a pretty close watch on his movements. Access had been gained to the room by a balcony which ran outside the window and communicated with all the other rooms on that floor. Three of them were empty. Not the slightest clue had been discovered, and although the Egyptian police, at the behest of Professor Fleming and the Cairo Museum directorate, had done their best, they had been unsuccessful in finding either the murderer or the necklace. Both had completely and utterly vanished.

The stout superintendent next turned his attention to a wad of newspaper clippings containing items of interest, paragraphs, tabloids, and articles concerning Mr. Janson, senior. There was a photograph of him which showed that he was a thin, white-haired man with an unlined face and rather large, deep-set eyes. There was a faint resemblance to Gary Janson, but it was not very marked. There was also a photograph of his home on Long Island and an account of his collection of rare and valuable antiques and pictures. He appeared to have spent a fortune on the acquisition of his treasures, and the entire collection was valued at the enormous sum of ten million dollars. Interesting, thought Mr. Budd, but not very helpful in finding the solution to the mystery he was trying to solve. It showed, though, that Mr. Janson was willing to spend almost anything to acquire any rare object that he coveted.

A detailed report of all the offences for which Karolides had been convicted provided a little better result. He had been arrested once in America on a charge of trying to smuggle a picture, which was known to have been stolen from the collection of Lord Hayfording in Berkshire, through the Customs. At the time of this arrest he had been in the company of a man, who had also been detained, known by the name of Harry Pollock, and described as of medium height, slim built, dark, and clean-shaven. This man, who for some reason or other had subsequently been released, cropped up again in another and later report of Karolides' activities. This time he had been arrested for receiving stolen property; the information had come from a police informer who had probably borne him a grudge, and Harry Pollock had also been implicated. On this occasion he wasn't so lucky as he had been in America. Both he, and Karolides, were sentenced to three years, a sentence against which the Greek had appealed and which had been commuted to eighteen months. This was the only time that Pollock had suffered a conviction, though he was marked on records as 'a very suspicious person known to be the associate of thieves.'

Mr. Budd scratched his fleshy chin when he reached this point in his researches. It seemed as if Harry Pollock might form a useful source of information, if he could be found. It was evident that he had worked with Karolides on several occasions, and was no doubt fully conversant with many of the dead man's deals. The big man sent through an order that the country was to be scoured for Harry Pollock and that he was to be 'pulled in' for questioning as soon as he was located.

Lew Glomm's record was very much more ordinary. It was typical of dozens of others. It couldn't be said that he had specialised in anything, but he seemed to have had a predilection for robbing large country houses while the owners were on holiday, or asleep. On one occasion, when he had been caught by a patrolling policeman, he had been in company with another man who had got away. The policeman, in his evidence, had described this other man as of medium height and slim build. Harry Pollock? Mr. Budd thought it was probable. If it was, then he had got hold of something. Karolides had been associated with Harry Pollock, and Glomm had been associated with Karolides.

It seemed possible that the three of them had worked together, probably under the direction and orders of the Greek. It would be a profitable combination if Glomm and Pollock had secured the stuff which Karolides subsequently disposed of among his clientele. No doubt Mr. Ahmadun was in it as well. The Sacred Ibis would have made a very useful clearing house. Mr. Budd decided that an interview with Harry Pollock would be most desirable, and almost certainly advantageous. It was more than likely that he knew where the rest of the necklace was hidden . . .

But Harry Pollock seemed to have vanished from the face of the earth. Every effort to find him failed, and then Jill Hartley, looking in the window of a West End store, suddenly experienced a revival of memory, and supplied the clue which led to his discovery.

PART SIX

THE MASK OF SET

1

Since her uncanny experience of waking up in the Ladies' Waiting Room at Waterloo Station in the small hours of the morning, without any idea of how she had got there, life for Jill Hartley had settled down into its usual, rather humdrum, routine. It was true that the persistent Richard Wayland had continued to ring her up daily, with carefully couched invitations to dances, dinners, and theatres, but that was the only thing that happened out of the normal. She continued to refuse with frigid politeness, but she found herself, to her intense annoyance, beginning to listen for the telephone. One afternoon he had failed to ring up at the usual time and she experienced an unusual feeling of disappointment. She told herself that the reason was only because the brief telephone conversation made a break in the long afternoon, but the excuse seemed a little unconvincing even to herself. She was determined, however, that she would not give in, though on more than one occasion, with the prospect of a rather bleak and lonely evening at her flat as the alternative, she had very nearly capitulated.

After the inquest on Karolides, which she had attended, and which was disappointedly lacking in anything sensational, the affair seemed to have rather petered out. Mr. Budd, who had not been present at the proceedings, had been to see her once, and questioned her about her adventure, but, since the only thing she remembered of that weird experience was stepping into the car and waking up at Waterloo Station, she was unable to add to what she had already told him over the telephone. The detectives were still keeping her under surveillance. She was escorted, at a respectful distance, to and from her work, and there was invariably a man to be found lounging aimlessly about the vestibule of the block of flats in which she lived. But no fresh attack had been made upon her, or attempted. She came to the conclusion, as the days went by, that the whole business would die a natural death, and that it was very unlikely that she would hear anything more about it. She was rather disappointed, because she would have liked to know what it all meant. It was rather like seeing the beginning of an exciting film and coming out before the end. She was curious to know why Karolides had been killed, and who had killed him, and what the real meaning of the Seven Lamps could be.

And then one Saturday morning, just as she was preparing to leave the office, the telephone bell rang. She thought that it was Richard Wayland, but instead of his cheerful, bantering voice, it was the more austere tones of Professor Locksley that came over the wire.

'Is that Miss Hartley?' he inquired cautiously, and when she replied that it was: 'Er — good morning, Miss Hartley, I expect you will think it strange that I should — er — ring you up. The truth of the matter is — er — I was wondering if you would care to come over this afternoon and have some tea?'

'That's very kind of you, Professor Locksley,' said Jill, rather astonished at the invitation.

'Please say 'No' if it will upset any of your — er — preconceived arrangements,' he said, hurriedly. 'I shall quite . . .'

'I haven't made any for this afternoon,' said Jill, truthfully. 'I shall be pleased to come.'

'Good,' answered Locksley, and sounded quite pleased. 'I'm delighted. I shall expect you about — shall we say — 3.30?'

'That will suit me very well,' said Jill.

He rang off, and she stood for a moment before putting down the telephone, with a little frown wrinkling her forehead. What had prompted this sudden invitation? Why was Professor Locksley anxious to see her? She set about closing the office — Mr. Tape did not come in on Saturdays unless there was something very special — with a feeling of intense curiosity. It remained with her while she had her lunch and during the short train journey to Berrydale. When she got out on the platform of the little station a pale sun was struggling through a thin film of cloud, and she thought how different everything looked now, to what it had on her first visit to the place. She gave up her ticket and came out of the station and a voice hailed her:

'Hello, Jill! Hop in!'

A car was drawn up in the approach, and sitting in it, grinning at her, was Richard Wayland.

'Nice of you to come,' he said, cheerfully. 'I had an awful job to persuade Uncle Cedric to telephone . . . '

'Do you mean to tell me that . . . that it was *you*?' she demanded.

'Of course,' he replied, opening the door. 'Entirely my own idea! I knew you wouldn't come if *I* asked you, but I was pretty sure you wouldn't refuse Uncle Cedric . . . '

She glared at him angrily.

'I've a good mind to wait here and take the first train back,' she said.

'You can't do that,' he retorted. 'Uncle would think it was terribly rude. After all, he *did* ask you, you know. It may have been at my instigation, but it was *his* invitation . . . '

'I . . . I think you are completely unscrupulous!' she cried.

'Say, rather, that I am a good organiser,' he answered. 'Hang it all, Jill, I had to do something. You turned down all *my* invitations, flat. What else could I do?'

'You could take 'No' for an answer and leave it at that,' she said. 'If you weren't as thick-skinned as . . . as . . . '

'A boiled orange?' he suggested, helpfully.

'As a rhinoceros,' she continued: 'You'd . . . '

'Boiled orange is more original,' he remarked.

'You'd stop pestering me,' she finished.

'Will you get in?' he invited, with a beaming smile.

'The trouble with you,' she stormed, 'is that you can't take a hint . . . '

'A hint?' he repeated, and suddenly roared with laughter.

'I've no doubt you find it very funny,' she snapped.

'Ye gods!' he gasped, helplessly. 'Is that what you call a hint? Heaven help the

304

person you start speaking plainly to . . . '

'Mr. Wayland,' she cried, stamping her foot. 'Will you kindly stop this tomfoolery . . . ?'

'I'll tell you something,' he said, seriously. 'You're the most insufferably conceited girl I've ever met.'

'Oh!' She stared at him, almost speechless with rage. 'Oh . . . You . . . you have the colossal nerve to say that to *me* . . . '

'Yes, I have,' he answered, calmly. 'Because it's true. If you weren't eaten up with an exaggerated idea of your own importance, you wouldn't treat *me* in the way that you do. You should regard the fact that I have spent so much time and trouble in trying to persuade you to come out with me as a compliment, which it is, and appreciate it.'

'I think you're horrible!' she burst out furiously. 'Nobody has *ever* spoken to me like that before . . . '

'Pity,' he said. 'It would have done you good, and saved me a lot of trouble.'

'Whatever trouble you have put yourself to has been of your own making,' she retorted.

'I agree,' he answered, 'but I believe there are the makings of quite a nice girl in you, if you once came down off your high horse and became a little human. If I didn't think so I shouldn't bother with you . . . '

'I wish you wouldn't,' she flashed.

'You don't wish anything of the sort,' he answered, coolly. 'You're really rather flattered, only you're too obstinate to admit it, even to yourself. You're terrified of making yourself cheap, and so you go to the opposite extreme. Up to a point your outlook is commendable, beyond that point it becomes merely stupid.'

'You are the rudest man I've ever met,' she declared.

'You probably haven't met many,' he said. 'People always think it's rude when anyone tells them the truth about themselves, because it's nearly always unpalatable. Now would you mind getting in the car? We can continue this delightful discussion on the way.'

She hesitated. Her first impulse was to take the next train back and leave this extremely rude and complacent young man to his own devices. But on second thoughts she decided that this might be a little childish. It would be better to meet the situation with as much dignity as she could command. Ignoring the door which he had opened invitingly, and which would have necessitated her occupying the seat beside him, she got into the back of the car.

'I should prefer not to continue the discussion,' she said loftily, and he twisted round and grinned at her.

'Suppose we call it a truce for the afternoon?' he suggested. 'We can't very well go on bickering in front of Uncle Cedric. He'd find it most embarrassing . . . '

'Very well,' she agreed, coldly.

He sent the car spinning out of the station approach and along the road towards Hayford Avenue, and during the short journey she stared frigidly out of the window and kept a stony silence.

Mrs. Moule admitted them, informing Richard Wayland that Professor Locksley was working in his study, but would be down for tea. Jill thought she looked worried about something.

'Give me your hat and coat,' said Richard, 'and I'll hang them up here. If you want to powder your nose or anything, Mrs. Moule will look after you . . .'

'Thank you,' she said. 'My nose does not require powdering.' She removed her coat, but retained her hat, and followed him into the big drawing room.

'You know,' said Richard, offering her a cigarette and lighting it for her, 'you don't know how nice it is to see you here.'

He pushed forward a deep chair and she sat down. The room was comfortable and restful, and she allowed herself to relax. Occupying the centre of the mantelpiece was a large statuette made of some kind of shining black stone. It had a man's body and a head that was like the great beak of a bird. It was a rather horrible, sinister-looking thing, and she asked what it was.

Richard chuckled.

'That's one of Uncle Cedric's special pets,' he replied. 'It's a statuette of Set, the ancient Egyptian god of sin and evil.

Weird-looking fellow, isn't he?'

She agreed that he was.

'That's the most popular way of depicting him,' he said, staring at the god intently. 'He was, however, credited with being able to acquire any shape or form he desired.' He recounted some of the myths associated with Set: the story of how he had turned himself into a black hog and torn out the eye of Horus, and several others. She discovered, to her surprise, that he could be serious and interesting. The clowning and the foolery were, apparently, assumed. He passed swiftly and easily from one subject to another, and the time passed so quickly that, when Mrs. Moule brought in the tea, she was surprised to find that she had been listening for nearly an hour.

'Do you take sugar, Miss?' inquired the housekeeper.

'Yes,' said Jill, and must have shown her surprise at the question, for she added quickly: 'Neither Professor Locksley nor Mr. Wayland have it . . . '

'Of course Miss Hartley takes sugar,' broke in Richard. 'Don't you remember when she stayed here . . . ?'

'I'm afraid I had forgotten, sir,' apologised the housekeeper. 'I'll fetch some.' She set down the tray and withdrew.

'I'll go and tell my Uncle that tea is ready,' he said. 'Excuse me, Jill.'

He hurried away and she heard him go bounding up the stairs. In a very short while he was back without Professor Locksley but carrying the sugar basin.

'Uncle is coming down in a minute or two,' he said. 'I met Mrs. Moule coming in with this and I thought I'd save her the trouble.' He deposited the silver basin on the tray. 'Will you pour out?'

'Hadn't we better wait for Professor Locksley?' she asked, doubtfully.

'He'll be here by the time you've poured out the tea,' he said.

He was right. As she was filling the third cup, Locksley put in an appearance. He looked, she thought, rather tired and wan, but he greeted her genially enough.

'I hope you will forgive my — er — little subterfuge,' he said. 'I was more or less forced to it by my graceless

310

nephew. It is very difficult to refuse anything to Richard. He's a most determined young man.'

'So I've noticed,' she said, drily.

'He always gets his own way in the long run,' went on Locksley. 'I find it saves a lot of bother to let him have it at the outset . . .'

'I hope you will take that to heart, Jill,' murmured Richard, with a grin. 'She doesn't like your statuette of Set, Uncle.'

'Not like it?' said Professor Locksley in surprise, blinking at it through his glasses. 'Dear me, why not? It is a most perfect specimen of ancient Egyptian art . . .'

'I think it's horrible,' said the girl.

'Oh, I see what you mean,' said Locksley. 'Well, you know, Set wasn't altogether a pleasant deity . . .'

He launched into a description of the place which the god had held in Egyptian mythology, which she found extraordinarily interesting. She could understand the fascination which the study of this ancient civilisation must have, for it was full of a strange glamour. When it was time to go, she felt that she had seldom spent such a pleasant and interesting afternoon.

Richard offered to drive her to the station, and she was glad because she could feel the beginning of a headache coming on. He suggested driving her all the way home to her flat, but she wouldn't let him.

'Well, anyway,' he said, 'I hope that this has broken up some of the ice. Perhaps, when I next ring you up and suggest an assignation, you'll consider the suggestion a little more kindly.'

The train came in as they reached the station and she had to run for it. She managed to scramble into a first-class carriage just as the guard blew his whistle and the train began to move. Her headache had suddenly become violent — so bad that she could scarcely see, and she felt a wave of nausea.

The lights in the carriage began to spin dizzily and a queer sense of numbness swept through her limbs. She wondered if she were going to be ill and, in the act of wondering, suddenly knew nothing . . .

2

She came slowly and painfully out of a world of blackness; not a blackness which was a mere absence of light, but a thick, treacly, *tangible* blackness that had held her tightly in a smothering embrace. She had fought this blackness frantically, desperately, and with an unutterable sense of *fear*. It was a blackness that was alive and malignant, and it formed a dreadful half-world into which its formless fingers were dragging her down . . . There was a horrible moaning sound, and a whispering of voices, and then, once more, the blackness enveloped her . . .

★   ★   ★

Dimly, like the wind sighing across an open moorland, a voice reached her through the blackness — 'She'll do now . . . '

★   ★   ★

She opened her eyes and closed them quickly against a blaze of dazzling light that seemed to burn into the centre of her brain. A voice, the same voice that had come floating through that terrible *living* blackness, said: 'She's coming round. The danger's over.' Another voice said peremptorily: 'More hot water bottles, Nurse . . . '

She opened her eyes again. In the haze of light, faces floated in front of her — strange faces that stared curiously . . . She sighed. Her head felt heavy and hot, and her body seemed no longer to be part of her. A burning thirst consumed her and she tried to ask for something to drink, but only an unintelligible murmur came from her lips. She felt unutterably tired and weary . . . Closing her eyes, she slipped almost at once into a long, dreamless sleep . . .

* * *

When she awoke she found that she was lying in a strange bed in a small, very clean and white room that had a queer smell. At first she was puzzled to account for this, and then it came to her that it was disinfectant. This was a hospital ward! She moved her head and looked into the face of Mr. Budd. The big man was perched on a small chair beside her bed, and he smiled when he saw that she was conscious.

'Well, Miss,' he said. ' 'Ow are you feeling?'

'I . . . I don't know,' she answered, weakly. 'Why am I here? What happened . . . ?'

'You're a very lucky young woman,' he said. 'A very lucky young woman indeed. According to all the rules and regulations you oughter be dead . . . '

'Have I been ill?' she asked, wonderingly.

'Very ill,' he replied, gravely. 'An' you can thank Detective-Constable Yelman that you're still alive. You was in a pretty bad way when he found you in that train at Waterloo . . . '

'Train?' For the moment she couldn't make out what he was talking about. 'What train . . . ?'

'The train that brought you back from

Berrydale,' said Mr. Budd. 'Don't you remember?'

She did, now. Recollection came flooding back . . .

'I felt suddenly ill,' she said. 'Just after I got in the train . . . dizzy and sick, and then everything went black . . . '

'You was poisoned,' said Mr. Budd, bluntly.

'Poisoned?' She stared at him in horror. 'I don't understand . . . '

'Nor do I, Miss,' said Mr. Budd, shaking his head. 'But I'm 'opin' to. That's what I'm here for. An' when I *do* understand it's goin' to be very unpleasant for somebody.'

His big, usually genial face was stern and uncompromising.

'How could I have been poisoned?' she demanded. 'Do you mean that I ate something . . . ?'

'Arsenic,' said Mr. Budd. 'That's what you ate, Miss. Enough arsenic to kill you, an' if you 'adn't been rushed straight to this hospital, it *would* 'ave killed you.'

'Arsenic?' she whispered. 'But how . . . who . . . ?'

316

'That's what I'm anxious to know,' said Mr. Budd. 'There don't seem to be very much doubt about who. It's the 'how' I'm not sure of . . . '

'I went to Professor Locksley's to tea,' she murmured. 'He rang me up at the office . . . '

'What did you have fer tea that nobody else 'ad?' asked Mr. Budd, and she shook her head.

'Nothing,' she answered. 'There were sandwiches and cakes, but we all ate them . . . Oh, yes . . . the sugar . . . '

'The sugar?' he prompted, as she paused.

'I was the only one to take sugar,' she explained. 'They don't take it . . . '

'Then that was it,' said the big superintendent, nodding. 'I'll bet it wasn't lump sugar . . . '

'It wasn't,' she said. 'It was granulated . . . '

'An' you take quite a lot in your tea, don't you, Miss?'

'Yes. A teaspoonful and a half usually . . . '

'An' how many cups o' tea did you

have?' said Mr. Budd.

'Three,' she answered. 'But you can't . . . '

'Four an' a half teaspoons of sugar, an' I'll bet half of it was pure arsenic,' said Mr. Budd. 'No wonder you was ill, Miss.'

'But . . . surely neither Professor Locksley nor Richard Wayland would . . . would . . . ' She broke off. Before her rose a picture of Richard Wayland bringing in the sugar basin. 'Mrs. Moule was just coming in with this. I thought I'd save her the trouble.' He had made the excuse of telling his Uncle that tea was ready to leave the drawing room . . . 'Oh, I can't believe it!' she cried. 'I can't believe he would do such a dreadful thing . . . '

'Tell me exactly what 'appened, Miss,' said Mr. Budd, kindly.

She obeyed, hesitantly and uncertainly, her mind filled with horror at the suggestion that Richard Wayland should have tried to kill her.

'Wayland, eh?' muttered Mr. Budd. 'H'm, he was out on the evenin' when Karolides was killed, wasn't he? He didn't come in until much later . . . '

'Oh, it's impossible!' she exclaimed. 'Impossible! Why should he want to kill *me* . . . ?'

'There was somethin' you couldn't remember,' said Mr. Budd. 'Something that you *might* remember at at any moment . . . 'E tried before, don't forget . . . '

Richard Wayland! She could see his cheerful grin, and hear his bantering voice . . . It wasn't possible, and yet . . . How hard he had tried to persuade her to go out with him. How persistent he had been in spite of all her snubbing. Was *this* the reason? If she *had* accepted one of his numerous invitations, would the result have been . . . this?

'I can't believe it,' she whispered, but she *did* believe it.

'Nobody ever believes that people they know are capable of things which they accept as a matter o' course in strangers,' remarked Mr. Budd, with a great amount of truth. 'It's only natural, I s'pose. Well, Miss, I think the best thin' you can do is ter go to sleep again an' ferget it. You're quite safe now, an' you can leave all the rest ter me . . . '

'What day is it?' she asked.

'Monday,' he answered, 'an' it's ten o'clock in the mornin' . . . Don't you go worryin' about your job,' he added, quickly, as he saw the dismay in her face. 'I've explained to Mr. Tape, and he says you aren't to think of coming back until you're quite well . . .'

'I feel all right,' she said. 'Only a little weak . . .'

'The doctor'll be here in a few minutes,' said the big man, getting up. 'An' he'll be able to tell yer when you can get up. In the meanwhile, just you lie still, an' rest . . .'

3

Mr. Budd rang the bell at 18 Hayford Avenue, and waited with mixed feelings. He was not under any misapprehension as to the difficulty of his task. He had no conclusive evidence against either Richard Wayland or Professor Locksley — no evidence, that is, that would have held good in a court of law. They had had the opportunity of administering the poison to Jill Hartley, but there was nothing to prove that they had actually done so. And with regard to their being concerned in the murder of Karolides and Lew Glomm, the evidence was even more vague. The big man was pretty sure that he was right and that Richard Wayland had been responsible for both murders and the two attempts on the girl's life, but the difficulty was going to be to bring it home to him. That was a difficulty that few people realised. It was not enough to *know*. Sufficient proof had to be forthcoming to satisfy a jury, and that was not always so easy. However, his visit this morning was purely routine. Jill Hartley had been taken seriously ill with arsenical poisoning after taking tea with Locksley and Wayland, and it was only natural that they should be informed and inquiries made.

The door was opened by Mrs. Moule, and Mr. Budd requested to be allowed to see Professor Locksley. The housekeeper invited him into the hall and went upstairs. In a few minutes she came back, informed him that Professor Locksley would see him, and conducted him to the study.

Locksley was seated at his desk, pen in hand, surrounded by a pile of books and papers, and obviously engaged in writing his history of ancient Egypt.

'Come in, Superintendent,' he said. 'Sit down. What — er — can I do for you this time?'

'Well, sir,' said Mr. Budd. 'It's about Miss Hartley . . . '

'Miss Hartley?' interrupted Locksley, in surprise.

'Yes, sir,' said Mr. Budd. 'She was taken

seriously ill after she left 'ere on Saturday, and . . . '

'Dear me!' exclaimed Professor Locksley, in evident concern. 'I'm extremely sorry to hear that. I trust she is better?'

'Yes, sir,' said the big man. 'She's better.'

'What was the cause of her illness?' asked Locksley. 'It must have been very sudden. She was quite — er — well, or seemed to be, when she left here . . . '

'It was very sudden, sir,' said Mr. Budd. 'An' the cause was due to arsenical poisoning.'

Professor Locksley gaped at him.

'Good gracious!' he gasped, after a pause. 'You astound me . . . How could she . . . ' He left the sentence unfinished.

'She was taken ill in the train,' said Mr. Budd. 'Ever since that attack was made on her I've had 'er kept under observation, an' one of my men followed her down 'ere, an' back ter town. It was lucky fer 'er 'e did, because, when she didn't get out o' the train at Waterloo, 'e went ter see what was the matter an' found 'er unconscious. She'd been very sick, an' 'e guessed that somethin' was queer about it, an' rushed 'er off to the nearest hospital. The doctor diagnosed arsenical poisoning an' they worked all night to save 'er life . . . '

'But this is terrible . . . terrible!' cried Locksley. 'How could she have taken it?'

'Well, sir,' remarked Mr. Budd, 'that's just what I'm trying to find out. I'm hopin' that you'll be able to help me . . . '

'I?' exclaimed Locksley. 'How can I help you?'

'The last meal she had was here, sir,' said Mr. Budd.

'Good heavens!' cried Locksley, in great agitation. 'You're not suggesting that . . . ? It's utterly impossible that she could have had any arsenic here . . . '

'She couldn't have had it anywhere else,' said Mr. Budd. 'She didn't have anything anywhere else . . . '

Professor Locksley took off his spectacles and passed a hand quickly over his bald head. He was obviously very much upset at the news, and Mr. Budd thought that, if he was acting, he was doing it remarkably well.

'I don't see how she possibly could,' he said. 'We all ate the same things. If, by some extraordinary manner, arsenic had accidentally got into any of the food, we should all have suffered . . . '

'I understand that Miss Hartley was the only one of you what took sugar,' said Mr. Budd.

'Sugar?' said Locksley, frowning. 'Ah, yes. Of course she was. Neither I, nor my nephew, take it. It is your opinion that the arsenic was in that? It scarcely seems possible . . . '

'Maybe,' said Mr. Budd, 'there's still some of the sugar left that was used that afternoon? We could tell then . . . '

'I'll ask Mrs. Moule,' said Locksley. He got up and rang the bell, and began to pace up and down the room with erratic, nervous strides. 'It's a dreadful thing to have happened — a dreadful thing,' he declared. 'I don't know what Richard will say when he knows. He's very — er — interested in — er — Miss Hartley. It will give him a very great shock . . . '

'To find she's still alive, no doubt,' said Mr. Budd, but he said it to himself.

Mrs. Moule came in answer to the ring, and Locksley made his inquiry.

'Would you fetch it?' said Locksley.

'An' the packet from which the sugar was taken,' put in Mr. Budd.

Mrs. Moule looked rather astonished, but she made no comment and went away. When she came back she carried a silver basin and a cardboard carton.

'Here you are, sir,' she said.

Mr. Budd inspected both carefully. So far as he could tell, they both contained sugar.

'When you filled the basin, Ma'am,' he said, 'was this an unopened packet of sugar?'

She shook her head.

'No,' she answered. 'I had already used some for cooking.'

'You haven't used any of the sugar in this basin since tea on Saturday?' inquired Mr. Budd. Again she shook her head.

'No,' she said. 'We have our own sugar — Gladys and me . . . '

'Who's Gladys?' asked Mr. Budd.

'The maidservant, sir,' answered Mrs. Moule.

'You brought this basin of sugar straight into the dining room after you'd filled it from the packet?' said the big man.

'No,' she replied. 'I didn't take it into the dining room at all. Mr. Richard was coming down the stairs and he took it from me . . . '

'Oh, he did?' murmured Mr. Budd.

'Is anything wrong, sir?' The housekeeper looked at Professor Locksley.

'No, no,' answered Locksley, quickly. 'We are — er — just conducting an experiment, that's all . . . '

The housekeeper looked unconvinced, but she said nothing, and at a sign from Mr. Budd, Locksley dismissed her.

'I'll take this sugar, sir,' said Mr. Budd, when she had gone, 'an' have it analysed. Could I have a word with Mr. Wayland?'

'He's gone up to London,' said Locksley, and his face was troubled. 'I'm not expecting him back until this evening . . . '

Mr. Budd caressed his chin.

'Pity,' he murmured. 'I'd 've liked a word with him. Oh, well, it can't be helped. Have you ever heard of a feller called Harry Pollock?'

Locksley shook his head.

'Who is he?' he said.

'Somebody I'm very anxious to meet,' said Mr. Budd. 'I'll just pack this stuff up an' then I'll be going. But I'll be comin' back,' he added. 'Maybe this evenin', maybe termorrow, an' I'd be obliged if you and Mr. Wayland would be at home.'

The words were mild, and so was the manner in which they were uttered. But underlying them was a threat, which Professor Locksley sensed, and his troubled face became even more troubled still.

4

The doctor allowed Jill to get up on the Monday afternoon. She left the hospital just after tea and took a taxi back to her flat, where she spent a quiet evening, reading, and went to bed early. In the morning she was quite recovered, and appeared at Mr. Tape's office at her usual time. There was a film at a cinema at Marble Arch that she wanted to see and, walking up Oxford Street on the way to the picture theatre, she paused to look into the partially-lighted window of a big store. And, looking, she saw something that brought memory flooding back. It was as though a cell in her brain had suddenly opened and let loose the elusive thing that had been worrying her for so long. Two minutes later, the film forgotten, she was in a public call-box and telephoning to Mr. Budd . . .

5

The stout superintendent was in his office, slumped a little dejectedly in his padded desk chair, and chewing on the end of an unlighted cigar, when the call came through. The analyst's report on the sugar, which he had brought back from Hayford Avenue, lay on the blotting pad before him. Nothing had been found in the carton, or the basin, but pure sugar. There was not even the merest trace of arsenic.

Everything seemed to peter out in this case, thought the disgruntled Mr. Budd. He had been forced to release Gary Janson through lack of evidence to hold him, although he was being kept under a close watch, and now, although he was convinced in his own mind that Richard Wayland was the man he wanted, it looked as though he would fall down here through lack of evidence, too. It was all very trying and unsatisfactory. He had never experienced a case that was so utterly incomprehensible. The few clues he had been able to collect led nowhere. Nothing fitted. It was all disjointed and without any connecting link: Harry Pollock might supply the link, but he couldn't be found. He had apparently vanished into nothing as though he had never existed. He was feeling weary and jaded, and more than a little depressed.

And then the telephone bell rang, and as Jill Hartley's excited voice came over the wire his weariness and depression fled . . . With increasing wonder he listened.

'You're absolutely sure, Miss?' he asked, when there was a pause in her spate of words.

'Absolutely,' she declared. 'I can see it now . . . '

'This'll want very careful 'andling,' he broke in, as portions of the problem began to arrange themselves and drop into place in his mind. 'You realise what this implies, don't you?'

'Well, no,' she confessed. 'Except that . . . '

'Well, I do, Miss,' said Mr. Budd,

grimly. 'Where are you callin' from?'

'Public call box in Oxford Street,' she replied.

'Get a cab an' come along to Scotland Yard,' he said. 'I'll leave word to 'ave yer shown straight up to me.'

He hung up the receiver, found some matches, and lighted his cigar. Leaning back in his chair, he eyed the ceiling through the smoke, and his brain was busy. He had seen the implication which the girl's words conjured up, instantly, and it threw an entirely different complexion on the whole case. The thing which she had unconsciously seen in the hall of the empty house on the evening of Karolides' murder; the thing which had been there the first time and had vanished when she had returned with the police, admitted of only one conclusion. It was a startling and unexpected conclusion, but it *fitted*. It disclosed a pattern which was quite different to anything he had anticipated, but a definite pattern all the same. And he discovered, as his alert mind played with the pieces, that the pattern absorbed them. He would have to go very carefully and warily, though. There was nothing as yet but an hypothesis. It would have to be turned into a concrete certainty, and that would require a certain amount of ingenuity.

Smoking thoughtfully, he began to evolve a plan, building it up slowly and carefully like a man engaged on a house of cards. And a house of cards was a very good analogy, for one false move might very easily bring the whole shaky edifice toppling . . .

In the midst of his cogitations came Jill Hartley, and for an hour they talked.

'There's nothing we can do tonight,' said Mr. Budd, at the expiration of this period. 'You go home now, Miss, an' I'll go on thinkin'.'

She went, followed by the detective who had been her faithful shadow all the evening, and Mr. Budd went back to his interrupted thoughts. All the rest of the evening and far into the night he sat there, huddled in his chair, smoking cigar after cigar, and when at last he roused himself and prepared to go home to his little villa in Streatham for a few hours' rest, he had perfected his plan of campaign.

6

'It is exceedingly irritating and inconvenient,' said Professor Locksley, frowning. 'I am engaged in most important work, and I am, at the present time, very busy indeed. I cannot afford to waste the time . . . '

'I'm very sorry, sir,' said the official from the Gas Company, apologetically. 'But I'm afraid we shall have to insist . . . '

'Surely,' protested Locksley, 'there are other ways? It is outrageous that I should be subjected to this — er — discomfort . . . '

'It is in the interests of your own safety, sir,' said the gas inspector. 'The main is very badly damaged, and there is the possibility of a bad explosion while we are repairing it. We cannot take the risk of allowing anybody to remain in the house during that period. It will only be for three hours . . . '

'I've never heard of such a thing before,' declared Professor Locksley.

'It is only on very rare occasions that such a necessity arises,' answered the inspector. He might have added, with truth, that such an occasion had never arisen before, but this would have been strictly outside his instructions, and so he refrained.

Professor Locksley tapped his fingers irritably on the top of his desk.

'What is the minimum period during which you wish myself, and my household, to vacate the house?' he asked.

'Three hours, sir,' said the inspector. He looked at his watch. 'Allowing half-an-hour for you to leave, that would mean it would be safe for you to return at half-past one.'

Professor Locksley considered for a moment, and then he shrugged his stooping shoulders.

'Very well,' he said, though his tone was not very gracious. 'I will arrange for the house to be vacated in half-an-hour, and remain empty until one-thirty.'

'Thank you, sir,' said the gas inspector, cheerfully. 'I am very sorry to have to put you to this inconvenience.'

He took his departure in the car which had brought him, and drove directly to the police station in Berrydale. In the charge-room, Mr. Budd was awaiting him.

'It's all O.K.,' said the gas inspector. 'The house'll be empty in half-an-hour, and they won't be coming back till half-past one.'

'Good,' said Mr. Budd. 'I'm much obliged to you . . . '

'Don't thank *me*,' said the inspector. 'I'm only carrying out instructions.'

He nodded and returned to his car. Mr. Budd went into the inspector's office.

'It's all fixed,' he announced.

Inspector Peel shook his head.

'I don't like it,' he said. 'It's most irregular. If anything goes wrong, there'll be an awful row . . . '

'Don't worry,' said Mr. Budd, 'I'm taking full responsibility. It was the only way . . . '

'When do we start?' asked the inspector.

'In half-an-hour,' replied the big man. 'We'll give 'em plenty of time to get clear.'

The police car dropped them at the

end of Hayford Avenue thirty-five minutes later, and Sergeant Leek, looking more lugubrious than ever, strolled forward to meet them.

'They've left,' he reported. 'All four of 'em — Professor Locksley, the young feller, the housekeeper, an' the servant girl.'

'Then let's get busy,' said Mr. Budd. 'You 'ang about outside, an' at the first sign of any of 'em coming back, nip in an' ring the bell. But don't let 'em see you do it. Hide in the shrubbery afterwards until they've let themselves in.'

He led the way boldly up the drive and round to the back of the house. After a short inspection, he selected a small window near the rear entrance.

'This'll do,' he said, and set to work on the latch.

Inspector Peel, visibly perturbed at this unorthodox behaviour, hovered uneasily beside him.

'We're breaking all the laws that were ever made,' he said.

'You've got ter break a few laws, if you want to get results,' answered Mr. Budd.

'Anyway, you exaggerate. We haven't tried arson yet.'

After a little while the window yielded, and he stepped back.

'You'd better go in,' he said, 'an' open the back door for me. I wasn't built to go climbin' through winders . . . '

Inspector Peel sighed unhappily, but obeyed. He scrambled through the small window and, after a short delay, Mr. Budd heard the rasp of a key, and the back door opened. He stepped quickly across the threshold and joined Inspector Peel inside the deserted house . . .

At the expiration of an hour they let themselves out by the front door, after refastening the small window and locking the back entrance.

'Well,' murmured the big man, softly, as they went back to the police car, 'was I justified in breakin' the letter o' the law?'

'I'll say you were,' replied Inspector Peel, fervently. He was a great picture-goer in his spare time, and had acquired several of these transatlantic expressions.

★　★　★

'Well, Miss,' said Mr. Budd, later on that day, standing in Jill Hartley's little room at Mr. Tape's office, 'you're willin' to swear that this was what you saw in the hall of 18 Court Road when you found the body o' Karolides?'

Jill looked at the object that lay on her desk and nodded.

'Yes,' she answered. 'I'd be willing to swear that it is.'

'Then I think we've got 'im,' remarked Mr. Budd, with great satisfaction. 'His real name is Harry Pollock . . . '

'The Mask of Set,' whispered the girl, and gave a little shiver.

'Eh?' exclaimed Mr. Budd. 'What did you say, Miss?'

'There's a statuette on the mantelpiece in the drawing room,' she explained. 'A horrible-looking thing — an ancient Egyptian god of sin and evil. It's called Set, and it was supposed to be able to change its form at will . . . '

'Oh, I see, Miss,' said Mr. Budd. 'H'm, very appropriate when you come to think of it, ain't it?'

7

For the ensuing two days the stout superintendent was a very busy man. He interviewed innumerable people, put through many telephone calls, and consulted a vast number of documents and records. The amount of sleep he managed to get during that period was less than five hours, and he was a very weary man indeed when, accompanied by Sergeant Leck, he drove down to Berrydale on the afternoon of the third day. Tired he might be, but he was conscious of a certain amount of elation, for the end of the case was in sight and he held in his hands all the threads. It had been a laborious and patient task to untangle them, but at last he had succeeded. In his breast-pocket was a warrant for the arrest of Harry Pollock, and he expected before the night came to have him safely lodged in a cell . . .

Once more and, he thought, for the last

time, he rang the bell at 18 Hayford Avenue. The housekeeper opened the door.

'Professor Locksley at home?' inquired Mr. Budd.

'Yes, sir,' she answered. 'He's in his study.'

'An' Mr. Wayland?' asked the detective.

'Mr. Richard is in the drawing room,' said Mrs. Moule.

'I should like to see Professor Locksley,' said Mr. Budd. 'Will you tell him that it's a matter of great importance?'

She nodded, and leaving them in the hall, went up the stairs. As she vanished from sight, the drawing room door opened and Richard Wayland came out.

'Oh, hello,' he greeted. 'It's you, is it? I thought I heard voices. Look here, how is Miss Hartley? I've been trying to get in touch with her. My Uncle told me all about that terrible business. How do you think it could have happened . . . ?'

'I *know* how it happened,' said Mr. Budd, quietly.

'You do?' Wayland looked surprised and startled. 'How . . . ?'

'If you'll come up to your Uncle's study,' said Mr. Budd, 'I'll tell you . . . '

The housekeeper returned at that moment to say that Professor Locksley would see them. They followed her up the stairs and into the study. Professor Locksley was, as usual, working at the big desk.

'Well?' he said, looking up over his spectacles. 'Have you discovered anything . . . ?'

'I've discovered everythin',' said Mr. Budd. 'I'm afraid what I'm goin' to tell you'll be rather an unpleasant shock.'

'I don't understand.' Locksley laid down his pen and clasped his hands on the desk before him. 'You've found out how Miss Hartley came to take that arsenic?'

'I've found that out, an' also who killed Karolides an' Lew Glomm,' said Mr. Budd. 'Mr. Wayland, on the evenin' Karolides was murdered, you went out just after tea an' you came back while Miss Hartley was 'ere — about three quarters of an hour after the murder was discovered?'

'Yes, that's right,' said Richard, with a slightly puzzled expression.

'Was that the only time you came back?' asked Mr. Budd. 'You didn't come back before?'

'No.' Wayland shook his head. 'What's the idea?'

Mr. Budd ignored the question and turned to Professor Locksley.

'You was working in here from tea-time until you went down to dinner . . . ' he began, but Locksley interrupted him.

'I was working in here from tea-time,' he said, 'but I did not go down to dinner. Richard was out, and I decided to dispense with dinner and have sandwiches up here. Mrs. Moule brought them up immediately after tea. I told her not to disturb me until Miss Hartley, whom I was expecting, should arrive . . . '

'So from just after tea until Miss Hartley *did* arrive, with me, you was alone?' said Mr. Budd. 'You didn't see anybody?'

'That is correct,' agreed Locksley. 'I don't quite see the point of these questions . . . '

'You will,' said Mr. Budd. 'Send for your housekeeper, will you please?'

Professor Locksley raised his eyebrows, frowned, looked at his nephew, and gave a slight shrug of the shoulders. 'Ring the bell, Richard, will you?' he said.

Wayland did so. There was a short interval, during which nobody spoke, and then, heralded by a tap on the door, the housekeeper came in. She looked inquiringly at Professor Locksley.

'The — er — superintendent wants to — er — see you, Mrs. Moule,' he said, and she transferred her gaze to Mr. Budd.

'How long have you been employed here?' he asked.

'Just over eighteen months,' she replied.

'I want you to cast yer mind back to the night the man was killed in the empty house in Court Road,' went on Mr. Budd. 'Will you tell me, as near as you can, what you did from tea-time onwards on that date?'

She considered, wrinkling her brows in the effort of memory.

'Gladys cleared away the tea things and washed up,' she said. 'And then she left because it was her evening off. I made some sandwiches for Professor Locksley and brought them up here, and then I went to my room and did some household accounts and read a book.'

'You never saw anything of Professor Locksley after you took up the sandwiches?' asked Mr. Budd.

'No, not until later, when I admitted you and Miss Hartley,' she answered.

'You didn't leave the house durin' that period?' he inquired, and she shook her head. 'If anybody else had, would you have heard 'em?' said Mr. Budd. He fumbled in his pocket and produced a letter.

'No, I don't think I should,' she answered. 'There is a radio in my room. I had it on . . . '

'Would you come here an' take a look at this?' said the big man. 'I'd like to know if you've ever seen it before. It's signed Cedric Locksley . . . '

Professor Locksley uttered an exclamation and started to his feet. 'What the . . . ' he began, but Mr. Budd cut him short.

'Be quiet,' he snapped. 'Will you take a look at this, Mrs. Moule?'

She came over, and Mr. Budd held out the letter. As she was about to take it, it slipped from his fingers and fluttered to the floor.

'I'm sorry,' he said, and she stooped to pick it up. Mr. Budd stretched out a hand, seized the grey, neatly-dressed hair, and gave a quick jerk. It came away, revealing a dark, closely-cropped head . . .

'Harry Pollock, I believe,' said Mr. Budd, pleasantly. The figure in the black dress sprang up with a rage-distorted face, and Professor Locksley gave a cry of astonishment.

'It's . . . it's a *man*!' he cried.

'The murderer of Arturus Karolides and Lew Glomm,' said Mr. Budd. 'A feller called Harry Pollock . . . '

'Look out!' exclaimed Richard Wayland, but Leek had been 'looking out' and seized the wrist before the hand could reach the pistol in the pocket of the black dress. The cornered man fought like a demon. In spite of his slight build, he seemed to have abnormal strength, and it took Wayland, Mr. Budd and Leek's combined efforts to secure him. At last, panting and dishevelled, the neat black alpaca dress torn, he stood, glaring hatred, while Mr. Budd snapped the handcuffs on his wrists.

'I don't understand,' said Professor Locksley, in bewilderment. 'What . . . how . . . ?'

'It's a long story, sir,' said Mr. Budd. 'I think we'd better postpone it until after we've lodged this feller in a cell.'

PART SEVEN

THE SEVEN LAMPS

1

Mr. Budd sat in the Chief Commissioner's office at Scotland Yard. Colonel Blair, the Assistant Commissioner, was present, and so was Sergeant Leck, looking a little uncomfortable in the presence of his superiors, and trying to make himself as inconspicuous as possible. On the Chief Commissioner's writing table stood six lamps, replicas of the one Mr. Budd had brought back from Lew Glomm's lodgings on the night of the murder.

'You have accomplished a very smart piece of work, Superintendent,' said the Chief Commissioner. 'A remarkable piece of work. I should be glad if you would give me the full story. Why did this man kill Karolides and Lew Glomm? What induced him to masquerade as a woman and obtain a situation with Professor Locksley? I should prefer to hear it in your own words rather than from the official report which, I understand, you are at present preparing.'

Mr. Budd cleared his throat, and his big, fleshy face expressed intense gratification. This was an honour that was reserved for the favoured few. The Chief Commissioner seldom took such a personal hand in a case.

'Well, sir,' he began. 'I don't know as I ought to take so much credit as you seem ter think. I was 'opelessly at sea most o' the time, an' it was really only a piece o' good luck that put me right . . . '

'It requires brains to recognise good luck when it comes along,' said the Chief Commissioner. 'Go on, Superintendent.'

'The greater part of what I'm goin' ter tell you, I got from the prisoner himself,' went on Mr. Budd, settling himself more comfortably in his chair. 'The beginnin' of it goes back nearly two years. As you know, this feller Karolides was a dealer in stolen antiques an' pictures — rare goods that was well known, an' had a history, an' couldn't be disposed of in the usual markets. He 'ad a sort of regular clientele among rich collectors who was willing to pay a good price for some valuable piece that they wanted for their collection, an' no questions asked. That was 'is main job, but 'e 'ad a few sidelines, like blackmail. In fact, he was a pretty good all-round crook. There was three people workin' with him — Lew Glomm, Ahmadun, an' Harry Pollock. There was all sorts of others, but these were the main ones. Pollock acted as a sort of 'finder.' He'd get himself a job as a servant in the 'ouse of a collector and spy out the land for a robbery. Ahmadun would find the right person to do the job, an' Karolides would dispose of the loot. Glomm was a kind o' general factotum, as you might say, an' had to do what he was told. He got all the dirty work ter do. The proceeds of any deal 'ud be split up, two thirds ter Karolides an' the remainin' third between Ahmadun an' Pollock. Lew Glomm only got a small bit, which varied according to what he had to do. Sometimes, when he hadn't taken any active part in a deal, 'e got nuthin'. I'm explainin' all this to give you an idea of what the Americans call the 'set up.' So far as this case goes, we're only concerned with one o' their deals

— the ruby necklace known as the Blood of Rameses . . . '

'But surely that was stolen over eight years ago?' broke in the Chief Commissioner.

'Quite right, sir, it was,' said Mr. Budd. 'An' Karolides and Co. had nuthin' to do with the original theft, or the murder of the messenger. The feller responsible for that was a man named Hakim; I got that information out of Pollock. Hakim stole the necklace in the first place, but it wasn't the sort o' thing that could be got rid of easily, an' there was a hue an' cry over the affair which forced him to lie low. Durin' this period he was taken seriously ill. He lay in hospital for nearly four years, and when he came out, still very weak and dying from an incurable disease, he was broke. At this time he ran into Karolides an' sold him the necklace for practically nothing. Karolides knew he had got a bargain that, handled properly, ought to bring him in a huge sum. The first thing to do was to get it out of Egypt. The authorities were still lookin' for the murderer of the messenger an' the necklace and, to add to the difficulty, there had recently been an outbreak of drug smuggling, an' all the Customs an' officials was more than usually alert. In a second-hand shop in a back street in Cairo, Karolides spotted seven lamps — them lamps that are on your table, sir — there was seven altogether, but I had to smash one ter find the ruby. They was of no particular value, but they would make a hidin' place fer the necklace if it was taken apart. He bought them, an' to cut a long story short, concealed one of the seven rubies formin' the necklace in the base of each. Six o' the lamps he sent to Harry Pollock, who had just fixed a job as housekeeper ter Professor Locksley, in the hope of pickin' up some information that might be of value to them. He sent them by parcel post addressed to Professor Locksley, bankin' on the fact that nobody 'ud be suspicious of a parcel addressed to such an eminent man. He kept the seventh lamp in case he should want a specimen of the rubies to show to any prospective buyer and prove that he was actually in possession of the necklace.

'Now, while he was contemplatin'
leavin' Cairo and returnin' to England
with Glomm, who was with 'im, he
'appened ter mention these seven lamps
in a cafe. He was talkin' to Glomm, but
he was overheard by a feller in the employ
of a man called Khyfami, who was
searching for traces of seven completely
different lamps. These were a kind o'
magical lamps that had belonged to the
priests of ancient Egypt, an' had been
hidden in a pyramid. Khyfami was
workin' for a feller called Harmachis, who
is a direct descendant of the priest whose
job it was ter look after these seven lamps
— the Lamps of the Gods, they was
called. When the matter was reported to
him, he naturally thought that Karolides
was referrin' to *these* seven lamps, an' not
ter the lamps in which he had hidden the
Blood of Rameses. He got in touch with
Karolides and offered him a large sum of
money for the lamps. Karolides, who
realised that he had made a mistake, but
thought there might be a chance of
makin' somethin' out of it, led him, to use
a vulgar expression, up the garden. He

stalled 'im, and when he got to England and saw Harry Pollock, he told him all about it. And Harry Pollock was able to give him further information about them. He had been nosing about Professor Locksley's belongings an' had come across an old book in which these lamps were mentioned and described. He suggested that Karolides should work a sort o' confidence trick on Khyfami — get 'im to pay over the money an' then do a vanishin' act. Karolides agreed with the plan. He was now in a position to substantiate his claim that he knew where the lamps were by describin' 'em in detail to Khyfami.

'He demanded a large sum down, an' the balance when he produced the lamps. Khyfami, bein' a simple sort of feller, an' believin' that nobody could describe the lamps unless they had seen 'em, paid up like a lamb, and Karolides made an appointment to give him the lamps an' receive the balance. In the meanwhile, there was a bit o' trouble goin' on between Karolides an' Pollock. Karolides had arranged to sell the necklace for thirty thousand pounds to one of his clients in America, a millionaire collector called Janson, an' he wanted it back from Pollock, or rather the six lamps that contained six o' the stones. Pollock refused to part. He'd got the stuff, an' if there was any thirty thousand pounds goin' he was out to collect the lot. Karolides threatened to give him away to the police, an' tell Professor Locksley that he was an impostor. Pollock devised a plan and telephoned 'im to come down to Hayford Avenue and collect the lamps. Karolides, thinkin' that his threat had worked the trick, went an' fell into the trap that Pollock had prepared for him. I don't 'ave ter tell you what it was, because you already know about the changin' of the names o' the two roads.

'Karolides had never been to Locksley's before, and when he arrived at the *empty* house, Pollock was waitin' for him. He killed him with a coal hammer, an' searched the body to make sure there was nuthin' to incriminate him. There was a letter from Khyfami about the Seven Lamps — his seven, 'an in his hurry a corner of this, with the words 'Seven Lamps', got torn off an' probably blew under the body in the draught from the front door. Also in his hurry he dropped the scarf he had been wearin' over his head — he was still in his guise of 'Mrs. Moule', for he didn't dare risk changing in case he was caught by Locksley leavin' or comin' back. As 'Mrs. Moule' he could always say 'e'd gone out to post a letter. He had to go all the way back an' recover it.

'In the meanwhile, Miss Hartley had been deceived by the same trick as Karolides. She went to 18 Court Road in mistake for 18 Hayford Avenue, an' found the body. Subconsciously she saw the scarf lyin' on the floor, but she couldn't remember what it was she had seen until she saw a scarf lyin' in the same position in the window of a big store in Oxford Street. Later she identified the scarf which I brought her from the room of 'Mrs. Moule' as the one which she had seen in the empty house that night. I also found shavin' materials an' other things which made me certain that 'Mrs. Moule' was a man, an' marked underclothing which told me he was Harry Pollock. But I'm anticipatin'. Pollock came back an' collected the scarf durin' the time that Miss Hartley was tellin' me what she'd found, in the police station at Berrydale. He also took down the false road names, so that when we went to find the body we was, at first, a bit confused. I think that's about all,' said Mr. Budd.

'I suppose Pollock killed Glomm because he realised that Glomm knew who had killed Karolides?' said the Chief Commissioner, and the big man nodded.

'Yes, sir,' he said. 'An' Glomm was scared. He was goin' ter tell me that night at The Sacred Ibis. Mrs. Grice 'as identified Pollock as the man who bought her the gin and walked 'ome with her. He killed Glomm to shut his mouth and also to find the seventh lamp, which Karolides had given Glomm to show to young Gary Janson, who was negotiating for the necklace . . . '

'Ah, so that's how *he* comes into it,' remarked the Chief Commissioner.

'Not quite in the way you imagine, sir,'

said Mr. Budd. 'I've had a long talk with that young feller, an' when I told him what I knew, he came clean. It appears that he 'ad no idea that his father was in the habit of buying stolen property to add to his collection. He found it out by accident and it gave him a bad shock. When he found a letter from Karolides he decided to teach his father a lesson. He tackled the old man with it and offered to go and negotiate for the necklace, but 'e had no intention of handing it over to his father when he had got it. It was 'is idea to make the old man pay for it, an' then send it anonymously to the Cairo Museum . . .'

The Chief Commissioner laughed.

'Not a bad idea,' he said. 'I wonder what his father would have said? Probably not fit for publication. Well, we don't want to take any action there if we can avoid it. Though if old Janson has been buying a lot of stolen stuff, he ought to be made to return it . . .'

'I rather think he will, sir,' said Mr. Budd. 'I've suggested to young Janson that he tells his father that he was caught tryin' to get the necklace, an' that the only way he got off was by promising that all the stolen stuff should be returned to its owners. If that's done there'll be no more heard of it, but if it ain't, the American police'll be asked to take action. Young Janson agreed . . . '

'I'd like to see the old man's face when he tells him,' said Colonel Blair. 'It was a good idea, Budd . . . '

'As I said at first,' remarked the Chief Commissioner, 'you've accomplished a fine piece of work, Superintendent.'

'Thank you, sir,' said Mr. Budd.

2

Karina looked across the table at Gary Janson, and her fingers played with the stem of her wineglass.

'You sail next Friday?' she asked.

'I guess so,' he replied.

'You'll be glad to get back?' she said. 'You always talk so much about America that I am sure you are very fond of it.'

'Sure,' he replied. 'Everybody's fond of their own country. You're fond of Egypt, aren't you?'

'Perhaps not so much of the Egypt that is, as of the Egypt that was,' she answered. She sighed. 'I shall miss you,' she said, simply.

'Must you?' he inquired, and the one-sided smile which she knew so well lit up his face.

'Must I — what?' she asked.

'Miss me,' he said.

'I don't know what you mean.' she said, her slanting eyes puzzled. 'Of course I shall miss you when you go away . . . I missed you before . . . '

'It's up to you whether you miss me this time,' he said. 'See here, Karina, why don't you come with me?'

'But how could I, Gary?' she said.

'I guess I could get the reservations altered,' he said. 'Mr. and Mrs. Janson. It sounds rather cute, doesn't it?'

'Gary . . . ' She stared at him with shining eyes and parted lips.

'I don't know how one goes about such things in this country,' he went on quickly, 'but I reckon you ought to be able to get married in three days. Isn't there a special licence, or something . . . ?'

'But what will your father say?' she asked.

He made a grimace.

'Quite a lot,' he answered. 'But it won't be about *that*. He'll have other things to worry him, I guess. What about it, honey?'

'Gary . . . are you sure, *quite* sure, you want me to go with you?' she said, serious. 'Quite, quite sure?'

'Quite,' he murmured. He put his hand in his pocket and took out an envelope.

From it he extracted a slip of paper. 'Take a look at that,' he said.

She stretched out her hand and took it.

'Why, it's a steamer ticket,' she said.

'Read what it says.' He pointed to the name filled in in ink.

''Mr. and Mrs. Gary Janson',' she read aloud.

'That's how sure I am,' he said.

3

The telephone bell rang, and Jill stopped in the middle of typing the long document she was engaged on and stretched out her hand for the receiver.

'This is Tape, Redman and Tape,' she said.

'What, *all* three of 'em?' demanded a voice.

'Oh, it's you, Mr. Wayland,' she said, frigidly. 'I thought you'd given it up . . . '

'You never thought anything of the kind,' said Richard Wayland. 'You've been wondering why I haven't rung up before, and when I was going to . . . '

'I've been doing nothing of the kind,' she retorted. 'I was congratulating myself on a little peace . . . '

'You know, your trouble is you suffer from delusions,' he replied calmly. 'I thought I'd leave you alone for a day or so, so that you would realise how much you missed me . . . '

'I haven't missed you at all,' said Jill. 'You should guard against this wishful thinking . . . '

'What are you doing this evening?' he demanded.

'I am going home,' she said, 'and . . . '

'Oh, no, you're not,' he said, firmly. 'I've booked a table at Romano's . . . '

'That will be nice for you,' she said, sweetly

'The table is for two,' he interrupted.

'I hope she turns up *this* time,' snapped Jill.

'So do I,' he said. 'Will you come?'

'No,' she answered, promptly.

'I'll be at the office at six,' he said. 'This really is your last chance, so you'd better think twice before you refuse.'

'Mr. Wayland,' she said, 'I will *not* meet you at the office at six.'

'Is that quite definite?' he said.

'Quite,' she answered. 'If we're going to a place like Romano's, I shall have to change. Meet me at my flat at seven . . . '

4

'Karina is going to marry the American,' said Khyfami.

'It was written,' replied Harmachis. 'And what is written will be . . . '